I0691377

NIGHT *and* DAY

Collected Short Stories

By

Andre Nguyen Van Chau

© Copyright 2015 Night and Day
by Andre Nguyen Van Chau

ISBN 978-1-941345-56-6 Hardback

ISBN 978-1-941345-55-9 Paperback

eISBN 9781311996503 Smashwords

AISN B016WM6OKE Kindle

Library of Congress Cataloging in Publication Data
Main entry under title: Night and Day
Library of Congress Control Number: 2015955047

All rights reserved. No part of this book covered by the copyrights
hereon may be reproduced or copied in any form or by any means –
graphic, electronic or mechanical, including photocopying, taping or
information storage and retrieval systems – without written
permission of the publisher.

ERIN GO BRAGH
Publishing

www.ErinGoBraghPublishing.com

Table of Contents

To the memory of Catarina Pham thi Vang

my Mother

And

to Sagrario Barbillo Van Chau

the love of my life

And

to my four children and their families.

ARRIVAL AT CHARTRES

But hope, says God, that is something that surprises me.
Even me.
That is surprising.
That these poor children see how things are going
and believe that tomorrow things will go better.
That they see how things are going today
and believe that they will go better tomorrow morning.

Charles Péguy, The Portal of the Mystery of Hope

So, once more, on Palm Sunday we walked, not all the way from Paris to the Cathedral of Chartres, all the sixty miles, like Charles Péguy did, but a mere eighteen miles from an obscure railway station, at the beginning of the plain of Beauce to the Gothic Cathedral.

Over four thousand of us, students, from freshmen to post-graduates, Europeans, Americans, Asians and Africans, marched in twenty groups, each group consisting of three "chapters" of seventy each, seven in a row, none of us adept to long marches, few of us familiar with tender green fields of newly planted wheat, few of us prayed with any degree of fervor. We marched under a miraculously blue sky, and a bright sun that had been pleasant at first, but had by degree become intolerably hot. We the pilgrims marched on, many of us urged on by a strange desire to make of this short pilgrimage a privileged moment, an experience that we would remember all our life.

1

We marched on without any short pause, encouraged by the promises of a lunch break by the roadside and a cool night to be spent in a barn three miles out of Chartres.

We chanted the rosaries. Then we chanted silly Sorbonne songs. Sometimes we allowed a song from a country or another to be sung. Sometimes we allowed prayers to be said in a little known language. But above us hovered the spirit of Charles Péguy, the mystic, the nearly forgotten poet, who wrote, and fought, wrote and hoped, who died a hero at the beginning of World War I during the first Battle of the Marne, a death he seemed to have predicted:

Blessed are those whom a great battle leaves
Stretched out on the ground in front of God's face,
Blessed the lives that just wars erase,
Blessed the ripe wheat, the wheat gathered in sheaves.

We marched on, all of us young, from eighteen to thirty, all of us eager to experience what would come next to our life, but old enough to have felt our heart broken more than once.

*

"I had to tell Philippe," *said Anne*. "It was not entirely my fault, but I had to tell Philippe," *said Anne,* rolling her engagement ring nervously around the ring finger of her left hand. Anne kept singing in chorus with her "chapter": she had to be focused somewhat as she walked at the tail of the chapter, and the next chapter that followed hers closely was chanting something else.

Philippe, her fiancé, was walking back and forth, observing the rows of students in his chapters and his entire group. Students were not good pilgrims; they fainted so easily under the sun; they ran out of water five miles after they left the railway station. As head of the group, Philippe had to run back and forth trying to figure out who among the rows of students would need attention next.

Anne looked up every time Philippe came back to her level. His blue eyes exuded confidence. They were hard at times, as if he suddenly reminded himself that he was in command and that he should not show any weakness. But Anne knew better. She knew that she could shatter his confidence and she could make him cry like a baby. And maybe what she got to tell him would shatter his confidence for good.

She had to talk to Philippe, even if that would jeopardize their wedding planned for the end of the month. She would not like to keep *that* from him. She knew *that* would be a burden, a burden she could share with Philippe now but not later.

"*Xesca* is a slut," Anne thought, "many people said so. Yet, are we too hasty in condemning her and ostracizing her?" Anne mumbled. "Who are we to condemn her that way? to reject her, to humiliate her? She is so kind at times, like when she stealthily drops a few new francs in the hats of *clochards,* like when she applauds an awkward speaker at her club."

The thought of defending Xesca, the Catalan girl, precisely on this morning, roused in Anne more than anger. She wanted to "kill" that slut. "Well, that slut nearly succeeded in..., oh my God!" Anne thought, feeling shame and humiliation more than at any other moment of her life. Anne allowed her shame to whisper: "Yes, that slut nearly succeeded in having me dishonored for good." The more she thought about what had happened the night before, the more she wanted to chastise herself: "Oh my God, I shouldn't blame anybody else. I got drunk, blind-drunk at a student party. It was

3

entirely my fault. By getting drunk at that get-together I more or less invited the men to trifle with me. "

She closed her eyes and saw herself in the dark living room when the lights were suddenly turned off. She saw herself desperately fighting off a young man who only minutes before he sexually assaulted her had been exhibiting modesty and decorum while chatting with her.

She felt sick as Horst's face appeared in her mind. His green eyes, his long and pale eyelashes that had never impressed her one way or another before he attacked her, now looked sinister and threatening. She should have been on her guard when he was around.

Xesca was the conspirator. Xesca had made the attack possible by turning off the lights at a *propitious* moment.

*

She *had* to talk to Philippe.

But Philippe was a group leader, so he kept walking back and forth, watching the members of his chapters. With a long staff in his hand, he looked like a shepherd watching over his flock of sheep.

"Philippe, I am one of your lambs, an injured lamb, when do you have time to stop and march next to me so that I could tell you about last night?" Anne thought, feeling abandoned, even when Philippe looked at her with his serene blue eyes.

Anne thought: "Maybe it would be better if I talk to him in the evening when we stop and rest at a farm. Maybe it would be better if I am to I talk to Philippe under the moonlight?"

She marched on with confusion in her mind and pain in her heart. The pilgrimage to Chartres no longer looked like a prelude to a happy wedding. She marched on, feeling the weight of her heavy knapsack.

*

Miriam and I were asked by Philippe to be the best man and maid of honor at his wedding. They were the perfect couple. Anne, native of Orléans, looked at times like Joan of Arc, "the Maid of Orléans"; even her hair was cut *à la Jeanne d'Arc*. Like Charles Péguy, the subject of her thesis, she was a devotee of France's greatest national heroine and Philippe, born in Paris, a pure Parisian, a *barbu* like me (bearded, doctorate-candidate) was writing a dissertation on Jacques and Raissa Maritain. He predicted that someday the Church would open the cause of saint in favor of Jacques Maritain and make him a saint. Lots of his free times besides writing the last chapters of his dissertation were absorbed by his work as one of the main organizers of the annual pilgrimage to Chartres and an executive of the Catholic Students Center that stood right in front of the Sorbonne.

He and Anne were inseparable, whether studying together at the Sorbonne Library, relaxing on a bench in the Luxembourg Gardens or enjoying a play at the Odéon. Whenever they appeared together somewhere, they looked like a royal couple, she with her radiant beauty and he with his elegant comportment and his air of authority.

They did not know that by being what they were they made enemies, who would love to take them down from their pedestal.

*

On that day, I was walking just behind Anne, at the head of my own group, my mind kept wandering. Earlier, on the train, Xesca laughed and dropped the bomb: "You should have seen, you and Philippe, how Anne behaved last night at our get-together. She, who claims to be so virtuous, so *sainte nitouche* (hypocrite and false virgin)! She behaved worst than the most dissolute freshman. I know now what kind of a girl she really is."

I said: "Drop that Xesca. Philippe and I know Anne far better than you ever would."

I looked elsewhere as I could not bear to look straight at her. On a normal day I wouldn't mind chatting with her because she was really a smart girl; but on that day, as soon as she dropped that line on Anne, I was frankly disgusted.

My interruption did not stop her. On the contrary, it seemed to embolden her. My refusal to hear any further apparently was misread by Xesca as a hurried attempt from my part to suppress my own curiosity. Oh yes, she was so clever at times!

Smiling sweetly, she said: "Somebody suddenly switched off the lights and we were plunged into the dark for a couple of minutes in Claudette's studio, just a couple of minutes... But you know what?, when the lights came back on, Anne was on her back, her white shirt unbuttoned, her bra gone, and Horst, stood there over her, looking dazed. Then he was pulled away from Anne and pushed out of the door by her friends while he kept saying: "I am sorry Anne! I really am sorry!" The smirk on Xesca's face told me she could have said more.

And she did. She shot her last arrow: "And you know what? Anne was drunk, drunk like a Benedictine monk."

I absorbed the poison, all the poison, before I reacted: "Shut up!" I said, "There isn't a shred of truth in what you've said!"

The poison worked as I descended from the train, feeling miserable.

Of course, I had heard about "groping in the dark", a game that many students played at that time. We were living in the 60's after all! The game was most of the times harmless and consensual. It stopped when somebody screamed, "Enough!" or "Stop!" But the game was never innocent and sometimes went much farther than initially planned. It was like strip poker that usually stopped before anyone got stark naked; but again strip poker games could turn ugly.

But none of the members of our Center would play that kind of games, none that I knew of.

I looked at my assembled group, my three "chapters". I inspected their knapsacks, their walking staffs, their flags and banners, and said: "Ladies and Gentlemen, let's start walking!"

But my mind was no longer with the pilgrimage. I walked at the head of my chapters at times, but most of the time I ran back and forth beside the chapters, watching the rows of pilgrims under my care, all the while worried for Anne and Philippe.

Miriam, my fiancée, sensing that something was out of order, came and touched me on my shoulder and for a moment I was at peace. But soon enough as she resumed her march in the middle of a row, the enchantment broke.

My mind was confused again. Each word that Xesca said seared into me. No, I should not believe anything she said. But, I was aware of the get-together the night before at Claudette's apartment because I was invited at the last minute. So was Miriam; but we declined as we wanted to walk together in the quiet streets of the *Quartier Latin* to where she lived, next to the Saint-Germain-des-Prés Church. With all the excitement caused by the final preparations of the Pilgrimage to Chartres the next day, we decided to take a relaxing stroll to Miriam's place. Now I wished I had accepted Claudette's invitation.

*

In spite of his apparently placid disposition Philippe loved Anne with passion. And reverence! As we planned our marriages in the same year, the four of us often went together to the *Quartier Latin* cafés, chatting far into the night. We also walked together in the Jardins du Luxembourg, or along the River Seine while discussing Charles Péguy's concepts of truth and justice. I wouldn't have been interested in abstract discussions on truth and justice if both Philippe and Anne were not so obviously and obstinately practicing those virtues to the letter.

One of the reasons why we were so close was that neither Philippe nor Anne would ever stoop to lie to us or tell us half-truths. They would sometimes apologize for not answering our questions; but once they gave us the answers, we knew that they had told us the truth, the unvarnished truth.

Miriam and I lived in a more normal world. We also cultivated truth and justice but were more aware of the need to protect our inner world against intrusions.

We were not solely interested in religion, literature and philosophy or classical music like Philippe and Anne. We liked to go to the Cave on the Huchette Street, a small place, packed with students, where we could feel the loud music penetrate the fibers of our body and reverberate on stone walls; we liked to go to the theater at night, and after a play, found our way to a restaurant at the Halles (Paris Central Market) for a steaming bowl of onion soup.

But we were so impressed by Philippe and Anne that we spent a great part of our time with them. Our love for both of them was deep and unshakable.

*

A shadow fell on me. I looked up. It was Claudette. She belonged to Philippe's and Anne's group just in front of mine and had slowed down apparently to talk to me. I held up my hand: "Xesca already told me," I said.

Claudette looked very unhappy. She said: "I apologize. I did not know that the Center was about to expel Horst. I was never close to Xesca, but when she asked me whether she could come, I did not have the heart to turn her away. I didn't know that they had conspired to..."

I said: "Claudette, you should apologize to Philippe or Anne, not to me. But you mentioned conspiracy..."

Claudette said: "Yes, they had obviously planned all that together. They had planned not simply to have some fun but actually to humiliate Anne, to humiliate her as much as possible. As soon as Xesca turned off the lights, Horst jumped on Anne. She screamed and fought and kicked him off. I found the switch and turned the lights on again before a minute elapsed. Just at that moment, Anne kicked Horst hard in the stomach. He staggered across the room and Bruno walked over to him and slapped him twice, then pushed him out of the door.

I immediately had a pretty good idea of who had turned off the lights; so I asked Xesca to leave, and she left."

Claudette nodded good-bye and walked away fast, to catch up with her chapter.

Miriam who had traded places with other students was now at the outer side of her row, close to me. She asked: "What happened?"

I shook my head: "It's a long story. I will tell you this evening at the farm," I said.

I felt utterly miserable. So, they had planned to humiliate Anne as much as possible, according to Claudette; and Anne was drunk, therefore unable to defend herself, according to Xesca. It was not merely groping in the dark for fun; it was really a sexual assault on an inebriate woman.

My chapters marched on, singing another silly Sorbonne song. The voices of over two hundred young students in my group did not synchronize or harmonize with those in the other groups. But they didn't care. They sang like there was no tomorrow.

I felt the poison of Xesca's words dissolving gradually, fitfully, causing pain then relief, then pain again. The picture painted by Claudette was too sanitized, I knew. The pain was somewhat dulled now, but did not go away. Whatever the circumstances, Anne was involved in a scandal. She was humiliated in a room full of people. Whispers would start and jeering laughter would follow her wherever she went. I shook my head, "Poor Anne, how could this happen?"

*

I knew that sooner or later Anne would slow down until she walked at the same level with me and then she would talk to me. There ought to be an acceptable and logical reason for whatever had happened.

My heart missed a few beats when she did slow down. Here she was. She looked miserable. She marched with me for a while before she looked up and asked: "Has anybody told you about Claudette's party last night?"

I said, keeping my voice neutral: "Yea, Xesca told me, and then Claudette told me. Two different stories, though."

Anne walked in silence for quite a long while. Finally she said: "I guess Claudette has given you a sanitized report...and I guess she will maintain that narrative when she talks to Philippe."

I was worried for Anne now. I said: "Philippe will explode even with *that* narrative. You mean that the truth is worse than what Claudette told me?"

Anne's face was crimson. But she faced me, looked me in the eyes, and said: "Yes, far worse. I know what Claudette told you because she had approached me early this morning and advised me to tell the story of last night in such and such way. But *that* amounts to lying."

I didn't say a thing but I thought, *Anne, be careful, your marriage may be at risk.* Then I remembered how fanatical she and Philippe were about truth. No, she would tell Philippe whatever had happened, how it had happened and why it had happened, without hiding even a little thing. I thought again, *Anne, be careful. This is life; this is not a philosophical discussion!*

Lowering her voice, Anne said: "I was *so* drunk! Yes, I was blind-drunk-- they all wanted to bring a toast to me for my approaching wedding, and somehow the punch, at first with almost no trace of alcohol, became stronger and stronger, with added gin, and everybody was a little tipsy, but I was way past tipsy. Seeing that I couldn't stand on my feet, Claudette came and asked me whether I wanted to go and sleep it off in her bedroom. Drunk as I was, I still remembered that recently there were young girls who at a party got drunk and went to sleep it off in a dark room and got raped. So I said no. Claudette then steered me to the sofa in the living room. I sat down and could go on chatting, though I could barely keep my eyes open. Horst came and stood in front of me. And we chatted. We talked about the pilgrimage to Chartres and about school.

Then the lights were switched off and Horst jumped on me. At first I thought that he was drunk too and somehow had lost his balance and fell on me. He giggled and I giggled. Then he tickled me and though I resented that quite a bit, I could not help laughing like an idiot; and he laughed too. But then he started groping. I was stunned and did not react immediately. It was only when he ripped open my blouse and tore at my bra that I became somewhat aware of what he was trying to do. I screamed. I fought back. I tried to push him away and kicked him but I was still under the influence of the quantity of punch I had imbibed; so, yes, I was awkward and ineffective in defending myself. While he was assaulting me, Horst kept tickling me and making me giggle uncontrollably. You know how ticklish I am! But it was not a game that he played. He wanted the people in the room to believe with my occasional giggling, that I condoned with what's going on. He wanted them to believe that I consented to play a filthy game of groping in the dark with him. I felt with despair his hands all over me. Seconds became minutes, I struggled and struggled, praying for the lights to come back and dreading that with the lights back everybody in the room would see me in my state of undress. I finally realized that he did not simply want to grope. I was terrified as I understood finally that he wanted not simply to strip me of all my clothes but to deliberately defile me. Something screamed in me: "No, that's not conceivable! This is not happening!" I got confused. I kept wondering why Horst hated me so much; why he wanted to humiliate me. Why he wanted to rape me in a room full of people. Then alcohol took over. I felt drowsy and had to fight hard to stay awake. A voice in me said: "You have to stay awake if you don't want to make it easy for him to have his way with you..."

She looked up at me and stopped instantly. Maybe she suddenly saw me cringe. She added after a long silence: "Then the lights were switched on again. Bruno and another man pulled Horst away from me and slapped Horst hard in the face, and threw him out of the apartment. Several others stood with their back to me to give me time to put some order back to my clothes. Oh, I was so ashamed; I really wanted to die..."

I said: "I hope you won't say all that to Philippe. He may not be able to handle it." I thought, *He would not be able to handle it because you have been for so long in his mind the image of perfection.*

I saw defiance in her eyes but she didn't say anything. Then she asked: "What was Xesca's narrative?" I shook my head, feeling like screaming. Finally I just said: "Bad, but not as bad as yours!"

Anne started crying silently. We walked on, but from time to time she leaned on me for support.

After a while, she left me and rejoined her chapter ahead of my group.

*

We stopped for lunch. Over four thousand of us spilled over the wheat fields adjacent to the roadside. For lunch time, people from different chapters co-mingled. Bruno found me and dragged me away from the groups. He asked: "You've heard, about last night?"

I nodded feeling his pain. If Philippe loved Anne, Bruno worshipped her. I said: "Yes, I heard from Xesca, and Claudette and Anne already. I don't need any more detail."

Bruno said: "That's good, because I don't want to revisit the whole thing. It was partly our fault, you know. We should have noticed that there was more and more alcohol content in the punch. We should have stopped Anne from drinking one cup after another. And we should have reacted quickly when Anne started screaming. But we hesitated because before she started screaming we heard her giggle and laugh... At times I wanted to intervene, but then, I heard Anne giggle again... Oh, my God, such a torture to me...Anyway, afterwards, I accompanied Anne out of Claudette's apartment, took her to the metro. I traveled with her to her suburban home. I noticed that she looked at the other passengers on the train with suspicion; she had never done that before. You know I travel with her every day, as my parents' home is a block away from where she lives. Yes, she looked at everybody with suspicion. When we came out of the metro, she stopped every time someone came up from behind us. I only hope that the fear and the suspicion are temporary reactions and that she would soon recover her fearless self."

I asked him: "What did you want to tell me when you took me away from the groups?" Bruno said: "Look, I know that my love for Anne is a one-way street. But I don't want her to be unhappy. So please make sure that Philippe stands by her, you can do that! I know you can do that! If he rejects her

14

because she is involved in a scandal, nothing would be able to save her."

I nodded but reminded Bruno: "This is between Philippe and Anne, you know, neither you nor I weigh much in the equation."

*

"Oh, there you are! I have been looking all over for you," said Miriam.

Bruno said good-bye and went away.

I summarized what I heard from Xesca, Claudette and Anne. Miriam did not say anything. I saw tears in her eyes. She stood up and walked away in search of Anne. I saw them sitting together from afar. They sat and talked until it was time to assemble for the second stretch of the trek. I had barely touched any food.

This time, Miriam walked by my side at the head of our group. At one moment she looked at me and said: "For the last two years you and I have found in this community a haven. We have felt safe with every member of the Center. Philippe and Anne have been with the Center over seven years. This is their haven. Now, suddenly something has changed. I heard of rumors of the coming "revolution" in all Paris. Events after events, issues after issues will probably destroy the world we have known and loved, including our Center. I have no proof yet, but I feel it in my bones. The world we have known will be gone in a couple of years. And, I am afraid."

I nodded; so many things had started changing. The population mix of the Quartier Latin had been changing drastically. There had been more clochards in the streets. More pickpockets on Boul'Mich (Boulevard Saint-Michel)! Students

15

at the Sorbonne were spending more time drinking beer than studying in the Library. Fewer people were buying books at the Hachette bookstores. With the events in Algeria, every day thousands of students demonstrated and clashed with the police.

Miriam said: "You need to talk to Philippe. Make him see that Anne is one of the first victims in our group – of a peccadillo? No, far more serious than that; it was an assault, a sexual assault, an intentional act to humiliate a woman - I am afraid that there will be many similar offenses committed right in our group, if we are not reacting fast and correctly." She sighed and added: "Permissiveness or absence of vigilance will destroy everything we have spent so much time building."

*

At the farms (at least a dozen farmers offered their barns and their dependencies for our annual pilgrimages), the men and women were lodged in separated barns and dependencies with hay-covered floors. We put down happily our backpacks, rolled out our sleeping bags or blankets to put claim on a spot. We sat down and took some food then dispersed into the fields near the farms and chatted.

I wanted to see Philippe before Anne talked to him.

I was not fast enough. By the time I was ready to go get Philippe, I already saw him and Anne leave and then I saw them stand and talk near an elm tree under the moonlight. I addressed a silent prayer to Our Lady of Chartres and waited. I waited a long time.

Philippe came back to the barn alone, somber and angry. I moved toward him when Anne appeared at the door of the barn and flung what I guess to be the engagement ring onto the hay-covered floor. "Then, take this back!" she said and ran away.

I looked at Philippe. I stared at him accusingly. He trembled like a leaf, then, as if he were waking up from a nightmare, he ran after Anne, shouting: "I am sorry Anne, I am sorry."

I bent down and picked up the engagement ring. I shivered thinking how fragile human love was. I saw Philippe catch up with Anne. I saw them gesticulate for a while; then I saw Philippe open his arms to Anne. I saw her hold him tightly while he kissed her again, and again until her sobbing stopped.

Later, he came back and asked me to get out of the barn with him. We did not talk for a long time. Then he said: "When we are back in Paris, please help us put the final touches to our wedding plan." A pause, then: "Thanks for standing by Anne".

The dull pain was going away. I laughed and said: "You may need this." I showed and gave him back Anne's engagement ring.

He hugged me and said: "You save my life. I have almost forgotten all about the ring."

I said: "You may want to give the ring back to her at the moment we finally see the steeples of the cathedral in the horizon.

Philippe smiled: "Yes, sir. That's a most valuable advice!"

We walked on for a while; then he said: "I was a fool. I got angry and I blurted out: "Why did you get drunk in the first place? Oh, how insane it was! I was blaming her instead of giving her my support. She ran away saying that our wedding is off. I still was angry and did not see how selfish I was, until she came to the door of the barn and threw her engagement ring away. Then, suddenly I realized how much I loved her, and how much she needed me. I ran after her and caught up with her. I held her and kissed her until she stopped sobbing, until both of us were whole again."

He looked at me and said in a monotone: "I guess you have the right to know what Anne said to me about the party at Claudette's place."

I shook my head: "Don't tell me anything, Philippe. I have already heard three versions of what had happened, including Anne's."

Philippe said: "I know that Anne did talk to you. She told me so, but she spared you lots of damning details, though. She said to me that you did not judge her but seemed to cringe at her "confession". That's why she had stopped short. She did not spare me even a little thing. That's why I was angry at first."

I said again: "I don't want to know more detail, Philippe."

The moon on the plain of Beauce was particularly radiant that night. We came back and sat near the elm tree where Philippe and Anne talked earlier that evening.

He said: "It hurt me when she admitted that she was really drunk before she got assaulted. It hurt me even more when she explained why she was drunk. Have you noticed how she looks when she drinks a glass of wine? She is always radiant; but whenever alcohol puts an additional glow on her face she looks *divine*. Sorry, but that's true. At Claudette's apartment Anne was quite aware of the additional glow on her face. She was aware that she looked more attractive than ever. She was happy and wanted everybody to see how happy she was. In retrospect, she said: "I didn't realize that I was performing a psychological striptease!"

I did not say anything. "Did he just take Anne a peg or two down her pedestal?" I wondered a short second. But no, in his voice there were only passion and reverence. I felt reassured.

Philippe pursued: "I got Claudette's version before Anne talked to me. Claudette did not mention that when the lights came back on Anne was half naked and that after Horst was pulled away from her, Anne seemed to be drowsy and could not even get up. She lay supine there for a long moment, without the will or the strength to cover herself. Some of our friends stood with their back to her to give her time to get up. But at the far corner of the room, the jeering had started, and horrid comments were traded back and forth. A loud voice asked: "Did you enjoy it, Anne?" Another voice said:"Of course she did." In the meantime, Horst was pushed toward the door while he blurted out: "I am sorry Anne. I really am sorry!" I guess he could laugh jeeringly or say some damning things, but he didn't."

He stopped talking for a minute then went on: "The story I got from Anne was filled with damning details. She was quite drunk and was only half aware of what was going on. She became gradually aware that she was being assaulted but did not know how to protect herself. Her attacker on the other hand was deft in his movements. He yanked her white blouse open and tore her bra away in a few seconds. She said she was scared to death and angry. She screamed and kicked and hit and scratched but he was too heavy for her to push away. She could not say with certainty how long the assault lasted. Claudette had said, no more than one minute. Bruno had said, two minutes. Anne thought it could be longer. She was unable to ward off his hands and she felt his hands all over her. As alcohol took over, she could barely breathe. She felt helpless. He had pulled her skirt up to her waist and her panties down to her knees. Horrified and paralyzed by fear, she screamed: "Oh my God please help me!" Suddenly her attacker seemed to freeze. He stopped even touching her. He got up and pulled her skirt down and her panties up to cover her. She felt great relief but still was exhausted and drowsy and weak in all her body. Then the lights were back on and two or three man started dragging her attacker toward the door. They threw him out as he said pleadingly: "I am sorry Anne; I really am sorry."

*

I said: "Philippe, you and Anne have been playing the game of telling it all for too long. Stop doing that or you will become intolerable; or life will be intolerable for you."

Philippe said: "You may be right there." He remained pensive for a while then added: "Anyway, I know that Anne is in pain. And I feel no other pain but hers."

I had seen her pain in the morning when she came to me. That pain was not going to disappear quickly by enchantment. For years, Anne would suffer in her mind and in her body.

For a moment I felt anger and hatred. How could an intelligent guy like Horst do something like that? I asked: "Does Anne have any intention to pursue her attacker legally?"

Philippe was silent for the longest time; then he said: "We discussed that quickly. We are afraid that a legal action wouldn't lead to any positive result. We are in a university world. The judges who hear students' cases have again and again leant toward leniency for the attackers.   "Boys will always be boys", they have kept saying. Anne was definitely drunk before she was assaulted; and that would not be in her favor. Then, there are liars among the eye-witnesses. They will give confusing accounts to sow doubt on whatever had or had not happened. They may shame Anne at the police station or at the court by saying that Anne and Horst apparently had taken advantage of the momentary darkness to have sex in a room full of people. It finally depends on Anne decision whether a legal action should be undertaken. She is adamantly opposed to such a step. She said: "I am already involved in a scandal, no matter what I say now. The scandal would be ten times bigger if I am to sue Horst for what he had or hadn't done to me in the dark?"

I felt revulsion as I said: "So, Horst would go free? He brought hell into the life of a woman then walk away without being challenged for what he did?"

Philippe said: "I should say that Anne does not seem to hate him. On the contrary, she said: "He could have defiled me thoroughly. But he had stopped dead on his track. He had tried to cover me up before he was pulled away from me."

I said:" Then the only recourse for us now is prayer. We all will need to pray for Anne to be strong enough to endure the memory of the attack and its aftermath."

We sat and did not need to talk any more. We just sat there and prayed.

*

Before daybreak we broke camp, picked up our crammed knapsacks, and leaving the hospitable straw on the floor of the barns, walked into the raw air of the plain of Beauce. *Salve Regina* we sang; and the plain of Beauce responded: *"Salve Regina"*. We intoned *Ubi caritas et amor;*

21

Deus ibi est (God is where there are charity and love); and the granary of France answered: *"Ubi caritas et amor..."*

Philippe and Anne marched at the head of their group. There was no more need for him to run back and forth as there were only three miles between the farms and the cathedral, and as no new problem was expected.

Miriam and I marched at the head of our group too. The songs rose and fell as we marched. The songs were now synchronized so that we all, the four thousand of us sang the same tune, at the same time. The songs carried far ahead of us and high above us. We marched with our flags and banners unfurled.

The early morning sun did not bother us at all. But we all longed for the minute when the steeples of the cathedral appeared on the horizon.

Philippe and Anne left their place ahead of their group and headed back our way. They joined us; and we marched on the four of us, feeling strong, and happy, and young.

Then the steeples appeared on the horizon. Philippe asked: "Anne, will you take this ring back?" showing her the engagement ring. She said with tears of joy welling up in her eyes: "Yes, Philippe, I will wear it as the symbol of our enduring love."

Miriam silently squeezed my hand. *The steeples, the steeples!* Shouted the pilgrims, *Chartres here we come!* With all kinds of flags, banners and pennants fluttering in the wind we advanced like an army of conquerors. Haven't we vanquished the night?

The shapes of the steeples became clearer and clearer. We knew we were marching toward the Cathedral like Joan of

Arc once marched at the head of her armies to the Cathedral of Rheims and the crowning of Charles VII as the King of France.

The emotions of our army of over four thousand pilgrims were brought to their climax when in the Cathedral we sang the *Te Deum,* waving slightly our flags and banners. The Cathedral was not large enough to give standing room to all of us. Some groups and chapters had to stay out on the Cathedral ground. But inside or outside, we felt God's blesssing as we stood in an immense crowd with one spirit and sang with one voice.

*

After the Mass the four of us lingered in the Cathedral; while most of the students were rushing to the buses that had been waiting to take them back to Paris. We were not in a hurry. We knew that the last bus wouldn't leave until all of us were collected.

We passed in review the various stained glass windows; then we found ourselves walking on the candlelit 13th Century labyrinth inside the Cathedral. Almost timidly Anne asked Philippe: "What do you see in the labyrinth today?"

Surprised by the urgency in her voice, Philippe improvised:"Today the labyrinth means for me our lifelong journey, from pilgrimage to pilgrimage until we arrive at the Kingdom." We walked slowly with tiny steps as if afraid to break an enchantment. Miriam asked me: "How about you? What do you see in the labyrinth today?" I said: "I see the mystery of life. I see obstacles thrown across our way. But with you I will find the way out. I see pain and suffering; and I see the end of pain and suffering. The candlelight assures me that we will not be lost forever in the labyrinth."

Under the eyes of the Blue Virgin and the Lady of the Pillar, we hugged the four of us. Anne said her voice filled with the strongest emotion: "I am purified. I am healed. The three of you have taken me back to the source of hope." Was she suddenly over dramatic? No, in the candlelight she looked *divine.*

For someone who had been victim of a sexual assault, just two nights earlier, Anne showed remarkable strength. Perhaps, the fact that she had seen us stand by her steadfastly in the aftermath of her ordeal helped her believe that the world was *not all bad.*

*

For Anne's ordeal to be over with after the pilgrimage to Chartres, however, the world would have to be *a world without evil.* Only three weeks separated us from the day of Philippe and Anne's wedding, but the three weeks were three eternities of humiliation for them.

The wicked tongues started embroidering on the assault on Anne. Soon enough stories of Horst enjoying Anne in the dark and continuing to shame her even when the lights came back on, were told and retold with increasingly lurid details. All the stories were said to be based on eye-witnesses' accounts. We saw evil in the raw. We saw the ugliness of human cruelty.

Our friends circled the wagons around Philippe and Anne, trying to protect them.

Strangely enough Horst reappeared, not on "our" scene but elsewhere. He got into brutal fist fights almost on a daily basis. He became insane whenever he heard someone call Anne "a slut". He maintained that he froze in the middle of his assault and stopped touching her when she screamed: "Oh my

God, please help me." But the more he fought and tried to silence those who affirmed that Anne was roundly and thoroughly defiled, the more uproarious the jeers and laughter became.

Many ventured to predict that Philippe, proud as he was, would cancel the planned wedding with *Anne the slut.*

The four of us stayed very close all that time. One day, as Philippe was discussing something with Miriam, Anne asked me: "Do you know what great lessons I have learn through this ordeal?"

I shook my head. Anne was crimson when she said: "I was on the verge of being violated in a room full of people. It was only by a miracle that Horst did not press on. The first lesson I learned is never to get drunk. If I had all the lucidity and the strength like when I am sober, Horst would not get very far when he assaulted me."

"And what's the second lesson?" I asked.

Anne became pensive. She said: "We need to know how vulnerable we are. A gust of wind can kill us physically. A momentary lapse of vigilance may cause mortal injury to our soul."

I insisted: "And what's the third lesson?"

She smiled while her hands trembled: "Love conquers everything. I asked Philippe: "If I were not only assaulted but raped that night; would you still love me?" He said: "I would cancel our wedding right away!" I paled; but he started laughing. He said: "Silly girl! Of course, I would still love you. Nothing could change that."

I stood up and hugged her. I said: "You are a very lucky girl. Not too many women meet a man who loves them like Philippe loves you."

After Philippe and Anne got married in the presence of hundreds of friends, the jeering and the insults came less frequently. Soon enough, the stories about Anne and Horst stopped being of interest to anybody. But some of the enemies of the couple kept calling her *"Anne the slut"*. The nickname survived for a long while. I guess that succeeded in reminding Anne, and us, of the three lessons she and we learned from that awful experience.

*

Two years later, as I strolled down the Avenue of Champs-Elysées one day, I met Xesca. I could barely recognize her. She was dressed simply but elegantly. Her sober make-up no longer attempted to hide her freckles, and the mute gloss she used enhanced the fullness of her lips. She looked most beautiful.

She waved to me and walked over to where I stood. She asked: "How is everybody? Miriam, Anne and Philippe, I mean. How all of you have been?"

I found it natural not only to answer her politely but to expand on our married life, as I knew that I was speaking to a new Xesca. She said: "I regretted very much that I left you with the wrong impression. But I really hated you. I hated you and Miriam. And I hated Philippe and Anne. You were so happy, so confident that life would grant you anything you really wished for."

Yes, I had realized that there were unhappy people around us who could resent our happiness.

Xesca said: "Two years ago you thought that I deserved my nickname, *Xesca the slut*. Right? But do you know that I had gotten that nickname exactly the same way Anne got hers. I was also a victim of a sexual assault when the lights were turned off at a party with a bunch of so called friends."

I felt a lump in my throat. I reached out and touched her hand. She did not recoil. She took my hand and held it. We stood there looking each other in the eyes. All the recent past rushed back, but its colors were different now. Standing in front of me was another Xesca.

She asked: "Would you like to take a cup of tea with me?" I nodded and we entered a lavish but quiet café on the Avenue. We selected a small table near a window. We did not say anything until we were served. Then I asked: "Have you heard of Horst recently?"

Xesca smiled and said: "So you don't know?"

I asked: "Don't know what?"

Xesca smiled again, but this time with some sadness: "You've never known Horst. You've only known Horst at his worst."

She paused; and I expected that she would take her cigarette pack out of her handbag. She followed my eye movement, and laughed: "I stopped smoking since last year." Yes, I knew how smart Xesca could be and how transparent I was.

She went on: "Horst came from a good Catholic family of Heidelberg. I met him the first week after he landed in Paris. He was a good friend and a good student. He seemed completely immersed in the study of French modern literature, with an emphasis on the writers and poets that were being called *"those hunted down by God"*, those who resisted God's

27

calling until God decided to hunt them down and pull them out of their comfort zone, or their labyrinth, or their quagmire. I know, I know, you and Miriam, Philippe and Anne have been reading the same books that Horst and I have."

"Yes, I didn't know that side of Horst and Xesca." I thought.

She went on: "One day, he fell in love with a Lido cancan dancer, a high-priced one. I saw her a couple of times. She was a gorgeous woman; and she moved in circles that do not include impecunious students, like Horst. Unexpectedly, she returned his flame; and for several months he was immensely happy. Then one evening out of the blue, she said she did not want to see him anymore. Imagine his rage! He started turning bad. He hated women in general and highly regarded women in particular. He wanted to hurt them, to humiliate them, when given an opportunity.

She sighed then went on: "Then that fateful evening arrived. He told me afterwards that he was trying hard to humiliate Anne as much as he could at first; but then almost immediately a voice inside him said: "Stop, Horst, if you defile this young woman you will be damned for good". He heard that voice distinctly, but he was suddenly sucked into a maelstrom of desire and despair; he saw himself plunged into an abyss and delighted in seeing his own destruction. Though the moment could not last more than half a minute he saw himself between good and evil, between Hell and Heaven, between what bliss he had always pursued and the torment he was ready to accept as punishment. He wanted to violate Anne and at the same time he found the mere idea abhorrent. He reminded himself that Philippe had a few days earlier told him about the Center's decision to expel him; why not take revenge? Then, he

28

reminded himself that Anne had never wronged him. He felt like screaming, his whole body wracked by waves of violent emotions. He wished that the lights came back to end his horrible dilemma. Just at that moment, Anne cried out:"Oh my God, please help me!" And he froze. He stopped touching her. He even tried to cover her up as much as he could. He did not defend himself when Anne's friends slapped him in the face, hit him in the chest and kicked him out of the door. Later, he craved so much to come back and see the four of you and beg for forgiveness. But he knew that seeing him again would simply add to Anne's humiliation and to your pain. That was why he left for Germany a few months later. Before he left he told me that it was Anne who saved him from himself."

Xesca's eyes were filled with tears. She managed to say in the end: "He is now in a seminary in Abidjan, Côte d'Ivoire. He wants to become a White Father, a missionary in Africa."

I sat there speechless. "Anne saved him?"I wondered. "Isn't that the core of François Mauriac's theology of sin? You reach God through your sins. Only sinners see the face of God when they stop sinning; and sometimes as we are going to commit the worst act in our life, God stops us on our track and offers us redemption."

We sat looking at each other in silence for a moment. Xesca seemed to understand where my thoughts led me. She said softly: "Horst read Mauriac ravenously. He did not know that one day God would play on him the same trick that He played on many of Mauriac's characters."

I asked her: "There is something else on your mind, please tell me."

Xesca asked: "Do you still believe that I was Horst's accomplice that night? Men are so blind! "Her eyes were cold and a little steely when she asked: "How many lights are there in Claudette's apartment?"

I said, not knowing where she wanted to go with her question: "I was in her apartment a couple of times. There seemed to be a light in the parlor, another in the kitchen, and a third one in her bedroom, beside the light in the toilets."

Xesca asked: "Could a person switch off the lights in her apartment all at once?"

Some light started dawning on me. I shook my head: "No, unless he or she flipped down the main switch."

Xesca was insistent: "Have you found where the main switch was located?"

I shook my head for all answer. Xesca said softly but convincingly: "The only person who could turn off the lights all at once was Claudette herself as none of us knew where the main switch was located."

I mumbled: "But why did she do that? Why did she want to hurt Anne? Anne and she were friends"

Xesca did not seem to hear my interruption. She asked again: "Who had the most legitimate access to the punchbowl that night? "

I admitted: "The hostess of the party."

She concluded: "It was she who poured more and more gin into the punchbowl."

As I sat stunned Xesca asked: "Anybody told you that Claudette brought the first toast to Anne's upcoming wedding?"

I simply muttered: "Oh my God, we were so blind!"

Xesca smiled sadly: "It was not entirely Claudette's fault. We all hated you, Horst and I and Claudette, and others. We hated you because you were so arrogantly happy. We envied you. We became more and more miserable seeing you so happy, so "invulnerable". Claudette was ready to pay dearly for a chance to humiliate Anne."

I slowly shook my head thinking about what Xesca just said and what Anne had told me earlier about vulnerability. I said: "You may be right there, Xesca. I wished we had seen, felt and understood more clearly our vulnerability at the time."

Xesca said: "Knowing what I know now, I cannot defend Claudette in any manner. You know what? She approached Horst – who had, according to some rumors, showed some skill in the game of groping in the dark -- when she saw that Anne was drunk, and told him that she wanted him to humiliate Anne when she turned off the lights. Horst laughed and said he had no problem with that. Then Claudette said: "You can even do better than humiliate her in the dark. I will keep the lights turned off as long as you want." Horst was stunned, he asked: "What do you want me to do to Anne?" Without batting an eye, Claudette said: "Enjoy her! Don't you see how alluring she is tonight? She is asking for it."   Horst was reluctant to commit a crime of that magnitude. He said: "Oh no, are you asking me to rape her? I will get at least five years of prison for that." Claudette said: "No, there is no risk here. I give you a

31

secret: Anne is extremely ticklish. You may do whatever you want with her provided that from time to time you tickle her: being as ticklish as she is, she cannot help giggling or laughing uncontrollably. With her giggling and laughing, anything you may want to do to her will be deemed as consensual."

I sat there, horrified, as Xesca went on: "It was Claudette who suggested to Anne to go and sleep it off in the bedroom. But Anne turned down the offer. It was Claudette who asked Anne to sit down and rest on the sofa. It was Claudette who waited until Horst came near the sofa to turn off the lights."

I gaped: "But why? Why did Claudette want to destroy Anne?"

Xesca shrugged: "Not Anne! She wanted to destroy Philippe. After that fateful evening, Horst did some research on Claudette and found out that before Anne appeared on the scene, Philippe dated Claudette for a while. Hell has no wrath like a woman scorned, you know! "

And we have trusted Claudette all this time! And she was one of Anne's bridesmaids at the wedding!

I had never felt so close to Xesca, I asked: "How about you, Xesca? Are you happy now?"

She looked straight at me and said: "I am studying now at the Catholic Institute. Nobody there calls me a slut. I stay on in Paris because I love the city. But soon enough I will have to leave for Barcelona to take care of my family business. My father told me that all my three brothers who work with him in our growing enterprise were perfect idiots and that he wanted to designate me as the principal partner."

32

"A White Father, a woman executive of one of the largest businesses and fortunes in Spain! Oh God! How things change! And how quickly they change!

I reached out again across the table and held Xesca's hand; I said with all sincerity: "Good luck to you, Xesca, my friend. May God bless you always!"

*

I kept the meeting with Xesca for a few weeks to myself or rather between me and Miriam. But at Christmas that year, I finally decided to tell Philippe and Anne about my conversation with Xesca. As I expected, Anne started crying softly when I told them about Horst's intention to become a missionary in Africa.

She said: "I have found the strength to forgive him totally. But now, what should I do to let him know that what happened is forgotten, completely forgotten?"

I shook my head: "I don't think that he entered the seminary simply to do penance for what he did to you."

Philippe agreed: "He may have seen God's face faster and more clearly than we do, that's all."

I told them about Xesca role's or rather Claudette's role on the evening. They looked at each other as if in the meantime they had found the truth, or had it figured out.

I told them how Xesca had acquired the nickname *Xesca the slut.* Both Philippe and Anne exclaimed: "How unjust we were with her!" Anne said: "I will find her phone number and call to apologize to her." I shrugged: "Here is her business card with her phone number. If you want to call her do it as soon as possible, because she may be on her way back to Barcelona soon."

*

Many years later, Miriam and I returned to Paris.

There had been many changes since the social revolution of May 1968. The French called it a "social revolution" because its political goal never materialized. Charles de Gaulle, another devotee of Joan of Arc, after some initial wavering, and a brief total eclipse, came back to power, stronger than ever before. The Communists' victory never materialized because they had expected a popular insurrection to overthrow the government. That never took place.

But the social revolution endured. Truth and justice, kindness and courtesy, decency, faith, charity and hope and so many controls of human behavior were gone. France had entered a long period where permissiveness was called freedom and moral values, obsolete impediments to the full expression of men's and women's natural desires and yearnings.

We revisited with nostalgia the Sorbonne and the Quartier Latin. But the Catholic Students' Center had disappeared. It was closed down in 1969, but the spirit that inspired us earlier was gone during the May revolution. The president of the Center and four other students were condemned to two months of prison for assaulting the police.

The disappearance of the Center saddened us tremendously.

We tried to find the *Cave* on Huchette Street where we spent time in a small space listening to music that reverberated against the walls of the cave. The *cavemen* at that time had been well-behaved and couples just sat and tried to hear the music penetrate their bodies and vibrate in them. The *Cave* was gone. But outside in the street, the *new and real cavemen*, the true barbarians had come and claimed it as part of their territory.

Boul'Mich was glowing with more neon lights than before; but none of the people walking on the sidewalk seemed to have the time for window shopping, or to enjoy strolling. They seemed to be in a hurry and they looked around them with suspicion.

The Halles or Paris Central Market was demolished in 1971, so, no more hot onion soup after the theater.

Anyway, one could no more walk anywhere in Paris after dark. The streets had become more and more dangerous.

But we knew that we would find a haven at Philippe's and Anne's apartment.

*

They had two children, Gilbert who was ten and Genevieve who was eight. The children were charming. They recognized us immediately as the people in the pictures we had sent to their parents. They talked to us like they had always known us. They laughed and screamed with delight while opening our wrapped gifts. Both Philippe and Anne had been teaching at the Sorbonne, but still were youthful and exuded enthusiasm. They were open to the younger generation and did not mind too much the "new freedom" of the students.

Yet their intellectual world remained the same with Charles Péguy and Paul Claudel, as their favorite poets, with Jacques Maritain and Henri Bergson as their favorite

35

philosophers and with Emmanuel Mounier as their political theorist.

We again, after dinner and tea, sat and talked about truth and justice, Charles Péguy and Chartres. For a second, we were overwhelmed by the memories of that particular pilgrimage to Chartres. Anne leaned over and put her head on Philippe's shoulder.

How much pain, and healing and joy, and recognition of life's dangers, and steadfastness of love and friendship were summed up in that simple gesture!

Philippe asked: "You mentioned visiting Horst in your last letter. How is he doing?"

I nodded: "So, I did visit him two months ago in N'Djamena, in Chad. I had started corresponding with him when he became a missionary, a White Father, in Africa. Last year he became blind, a victim of River Blindness or onchocerciasis."

Anne paled. Her voice trembled as she asked: "Is the blindness temporary?"

I shook my head: "There seems to be no way he could recuperate his vision. He has accepted the verdict. He simply said that now he cannot see people but he can still talk to them and listen to them; and he thanks God for that!"

I added as I saw tears welling up in Anne's eyes: "Though blind he smiled all the time. He said he had finally found peace. He explained to me that N'Djamena meant "resting place". He asked me to tell you that he was sorry, had been sorry for the last twelve years. He asked for your forgiveness."

Anne burst into tears. She said: "I have forgiven him a long time ago when you told me that Horst was in a seminary and that he wanted to be a missionary in Africa."

Philippe said: "We even wrote a special prayer that we said every evening for him. Thank you for visiting him. If you see him again, please ask him to pray for us."

I knew then that both of them had truly forgiven Horst. We stood up and hugged the four of us for a long time.

I looked at Miriam. She was radiant.

We just came out of a terrible war. We had seen the world of our mature adulthood being swallowed by a cataclysm before our eyes.

We had just seen the world of our youth, the Paris that we loved so much, no longer there. But for a moment, that evening, seeing the quiet happiness of our friends we warmed up to the new world that managed to leave alone islands of beatitudes.

No matter how many changes had occurred in Paris, something remained unchanged. For a moment Paris became again our little village. For a moment, we were at peace again.

AUTOPSY OF A SUICIDE

She gave us joy and ecstasy. She gave us unimaginable and inhuman pleasure. She gave us pain. She gave us damnation. She gave us redemption and peace. She gives us divine peace.

She gives us life. She gives us the hope that one day we will see *her* again and to be with *her* again, forever.

*

Hoang is dead, dead for good. She jumped in front of a moving truck ten days ago. The gorgeous and radiant girl with phoenix eyes and jade white hands! She was all joy and happiness. We do not understand! We couldn't understand why a young woman like her would one day, out of the blue, decide to commit suicide.

Let's get back to the starting point.

But there is no starting point! For us now the beginnings appear hazy at best. We are no longer certain about how she first joined our group. Our memory plays tricks on us when we try to focus on any point along the axis of time that started from nowhere and is not going to end anywhere. Was she seven, or eight or nine when she threw her lot in with our goalless, rowdy bunch of misfits?

If we could trust our memory somewhat we would say that she was quite plain as a girl at the time. None of us paid

39

much attention to her appearance. Like boys our age, we preferred to stay away from girls. We tolerated her because we could not get rid of her. She was a skinny girl with exceedingly large brown eyes and long legs. If we stopped to look at her at all, it was because of her eyes. She was a tomboy and she followed us into all kinds of games requiring physical strength or senseless intrepidity. She had no fear and no qualms in wrestling with us or rolling downhill in a barrel with us, or jumping into a stream with us, coming out of the water with wet clothes and drying herself like we did by lying on the grass under the summer sun.

For the first couple of years, at good moments we counted her as just one more guy; at bad moments, we saw in her a burden.

When she was ten she became depressed for weeks and stopped playing with us. Then she shook off her depression and became a laughing tomboy again. But we noticed that she began avoiding any physical contact with us. Except when we climbed up vertical boulders, she routinely refused our helping hand. If she had to cross a stream, she would jump from rock to rock ignoring our offered help. No more wrestling, no more barrel rolling, no more jumping on us and making us carry her on our shoulders.

We continued to have fun with her in our midst, though. We grew up like that, not seeing that the skinny girl with big eyes had gradually changed into a beauty. And then suddenly one day we started blushing when we saw her coming and knew that she made our heart beat faster and our life more meaningful by simply appearing on the scene. From then on we no longer made gross jokes, or talked nonsensically, or played dirty tricks on one another. She was there and we better behaved.

The bunch of unruly kids underwent a radical metamorphosis. We talked politely, dressed tastefully, observed long silences at times and tried hard to show some degree of maturity.

We were twelve and thought that someday soon we would come out of our shell and declare our love to her and if she said yes, go out and conquer the world.

Oh God, we would give an arm and a leg to be alone with her for an hour, even if during that hour we would not dare look at her or say anything to her. Yes, we would die to buy an hour alone with her to simply sense her closeness. But we were never alone with her. She was always with the four of us.

We soon knew that we would never declare our love to her. What for anyway?

We were so perfectly happy like that, with her no longer tagging along, but being the center of the group. Why should we change that? We were inseparable. We were called The Queen and her Four Musketeers, or more ironically, Queen Bee and her Four Drones. We had no problem with that. We believed that we had bought the winning lottery ticket, that we had won the jackpot. We had everything that we had wished for, because she was there, all the time with the four of us.

The skinny girl had become an enchantment that we shared between the four of us. We somehow came to believe that our precarious and weird group of five would last forever, with the four of us as planets circling around her, the fixed star, in the middle.

Then cataclysmic events took place in 1945. We were thirteen years old by that time. Revolution, war, the Japanese coup de force, the detention centers for the French, including

41

the civilians, the return of the French, the return of peace and order, the final departure of the French, all those events changed the world all around us but did not change our way of life.

We enjoyed being out of school in early 1945. With all the schools closed, we spent glorious days exploring Dalat's natural beauties, visiting all the waterfalls, the plantations along the highway that led from our foggy city to Saigon, camping in remote forests and on inaccessible mountains, drinking water that came out of the rocks challenging all the freshwater amoeba species.

Fear seized us for a while when the Japanese put most of the French population in detention camps, as Alain, one of us, was French. But fortunately Dr. Mirot, Alain's Dad, was not disturbed because he owned and ran rubber plantations that were declared by Japanese as of vital importance to the Greater Japan's continued war efforts.

So we went through the upheavals with our group unscathed.

Then the schools reopened. We resumed our pre-revolution routine.

We continued to live in a cocoon created by our strange friendship. The cocoon sheltered us and for the next ten years: nothing new ever came to disturb our dream world, even though five years after the Revolution, we graduated from high school.

We were eighteen at that time. We all decided not to go to college in Saigon. Hoang worked in an office, handling her parents' lumber business; Alain started as a manager of one of his parents' plantations; Tan managed his Dad's pharmacy in Dalat, and Cuong worked with his parents on their truck farm in Saint-Jean Parish. I sat down and started working laboriously on my first book about Eastern philosophy, while teaching at a private elementary school.

Though having responsibilities now, we got together as often and as long as we could and the activities of our gang of five remained our principal focus.

With every passing year, each one of us took on more responsibilities in the world around us. I became a lecturer on Oriental Philosophy at the newly created Dalat University in 1957; Alain became general manager of his parents' coffee, tea and rubber plantations; Tan actually ran all his Dad's pharmacies in Dalat and Nha Trang; Cuong joined the National Military Academy and soon became the adjutant of the General Commander of the Academy; and Hoang apparently ran all the saw mills and the lumber business of her parents.

Some strange and new things occurred in our group though. We noticed that Hoang became more and more possessive. She resented any young girl who came near us. She did not mind showing that she was jealous. And when she fought, she fought like a tigress. We were amazed. We had no intention of getting to know anybody outside our group. And certainly we would never imagine that we would befriend another girl.

Did Hoang appreciate our friendship to that degree? Did she believe for one moment that any one of us would be interested in somebody else? We had always thought that we needed her far more than she needed us.

*

Then one day, without any warning, without any preliminary, Hoang announced to us that she was about to get married with someone outside of our group. It was in early 1958, when we were twenty-six.

We were stunned. We felt betrayed. We went through denial, anger, depression and reluctant acceptance, all the various stages that one experiences when faced with the death of a loved one. We did not know how to handle that catastrophe.

Sure, we were twenty-six and we had started each one a different but respectable career; yet we still were a bunch of young men who had not outgrown their childhood or adolescence.

Yet that did not prevent us from feeling the full impact of that mortal blow. We turned to one another in total confusion. We asked: "What happened? Why did this happen?" The familiar world crumbled in front of our eyes and we were left to wander over the ruins of our youth, and to foresee the empty days and nights for the rest of our life.

We decreed that we should do something to reverse her decision or her parents' decision. Indeed, at first we thought that the decision must have come from her parents. But that couldn't be. Hoang had always been independent and we had never seen or heard Mr. or Mrs. Cuong give her an order. No, the decision was Hoang's and Hoang's alone.

We wanted to see that decision reversed but none of us had the courage to do anything about that. We were paralyzed, frozen, and unable to make the slightest move.

We met and discussed the matter night and day. We analyzed Hoang's every word, every gesture in the days, weeks and months leading to her surprising announcement.

Before the announcement we had often seen her cry when she thought we were not looking. At times, she screamed angrily: "Why don't you go and try to make other friends? Why don't you think about founding a family? All of you are more than twenty-five year old already. Why don't you try to get married?"

Remembering that in the not distant past she had made a scene if we just had a trivial conversation with another young girl, we could only shake our head in disbelief.

*

She did come to me two months before the wedding. But I shouldn't say anything about that.

Then the wedding came. Ironically, her parents insisted on our attendance. They emphasized the important role we had played on her growing up. They even ventured to say that her husband, Phap, would be dismayed and offended if we chose not to show up.

Their wedding night! The four of us walked along the banks of The Great Lake (Grand Lac). None of us said anything. We knew that our lives had ended before they even began. We knew that we would not find real solace even in the company of each other.

It was a cold night in Dalat. Wrapped in our thick overcoat we walked on. It would be a blessing if one of us could cry or sob. But none of us cried, none of us sobbed. The bunch of kids had suddenly mutated into men.

We all understood that Phap, her husband, had more to offer to Hoang materially than anyone of us. His family was extremely wealthy with immense rice fields in the Delta. His parents were the proud owners of two dozen villas on the most

45

elegant streets in Saigon. They even had an apartment in Paris and a mansion in Cannes, Southern France. Phap was offered one of the villas in Saigon as a wedding gift. Phap himself was a famous physician with an elite clientele; he loved traveling, sailing, skiing; and he spoke fluently at least five languages.

The only shortcoming we could see in him was his mouth. His infrequent smiles always ended up with a grin. It was a tic that he apparently could not suppress. He also had exceedingly large eyes like Hoang when she was very young; but his eyes were enlarged with the heavy short-sighted glasses he wore. Maybe his voice was a bit too rasping to be pleasant. But, who is perfect anyway? He had beaten us collectively and individually. Though we did not hate him, we knew that he had made our lives miserable. We envied him, of course, for two long years.

We did not know what we would do with the rest of our life. I immersed myself into the study of Zhuangzi. Alain stayed for long periods in Dat Do, in the villa he built and used as office in his coffee plantation there. Tan traveled to his pharmacy in Nha Trang more and more frequently. Cuong was no longer an adjutant. He became an instructor at the full-fledged National Military Academy.

We still met frequently and were as close as we had been before Hoang's marriage. But we knew we had changed, radically. We knew that Alain went to church on a regular basis now. Apparently, he tried to find solace in religion. So did Tan who visited and stayed long hours at the old Linh Son Pagoda, built in 1938 to meditate. We noted that Cuong, who since childhood had been a devoted Christian, went to mass early everyday at the Cathedral. I, for my part, remained an atheist in daytime, but could not help praying for relief during my long sleepless nights.

We were in mourning until one day Hoang came back to us and spent two glorious weeks with us. She went back to Dalat without her husband. And she spent most of her time with us. She laughed a lot, racing with us on the paddleboats on The Great Lake, or diving with us into the heated swimming pool of her parents' villa.

We inquired politely once about Phap, her husband. But when she responded with a frown we decided not to ask again. We were as happy as we could be. Within a few days we gathered thousands of memories to last a lifetime. Stupidly happy as we were, we still found her joy to be a little artificial, her laughter a little forced, even her flirting with us a little strange.

Two weeks went by quickly; then one day she jumped in front of a moving truck.

*

Alain drove us to the Gougah Falls. He looked grim like the days three years earlier when Irene, his mother, passed away.

The fact that Alain was French did not distinguish him from us. Alain had always been one of us. He spoke Vietnamese without an accent. He remembered every line in *Kim Van Kieu,* the Vietnamese ultimate classic. He behaved like a Vietnamese since his childhood.

Alain drove us to the Gougah Falls ten days after we buried Hoang and fifteen days after she died. He drove like a maniac. We didn't care. We would welcome death! Any kind of death! She had been our love and our life. How could she die? How could a goddess die?

Did her husband drive her to suicide? Did Phap cause her death?

Because of him Hoang had completely disappeared from our world for two years. Not a letter, not a phone call. Absolutely nothing! Was she so enamored with him that she forgot all about us?

Two months before Hoang's suicide, we couldn't stand that silence any more. We sent Tan to Saigon.

Tan's father owned the largest pharmacies in Dalat and Nha Trang at the time. He had a winter residence in Saigon on Pasteur Street, not far from Phap's villa. Though it was still summer we asked Tan to go to Saigon. Tan didn't mind.

His father, Dr. Thieu and his mother after thirty years of happy married life were then separated. The winter home in Saigon was left vacant. But Tan didn't mind to go there. He recorded in his diary all the chance meetings he had with Hoang and Phap. Chance meetings only, as neither Hoang nor Phap invited Tan to their home, and Tan never dared drop by to say hello. Tan had always been shy when it came to Hoang. We surmised that he would run to her in a hurry if she ever lifted a finger and beckoned to him. But he would never initiate anything, preferring to watch her from a distance. His comportment with Phap, the husband, was curt, bordering on discourteous. Probably that was the reason why neither Phap nor Hoang invited Tan to their home.

So, though he was their neighbor for two months, he did not say more than a dozen words to Hoang but continued to jot down in his diary long paragraphs every time he ran into her or her husband.

When he returned to Dalat in the fall, he showed us his diary. Reading his diary was like reading our own confessions.

We were both excited when he mentioned Hoang and a little ashamed of ourselves as if we were collectively exposing ourselves.

We never thought at the time that one day Hoang would walk back into our lives and play and laugh and flirt with us as if her marriage with Phap had been one of our bad dreams and that in reality she had never left us; as if nothing had happened.

*

Here we were: on top of the Gougah falls.

The first autumn rains had added volume to the streams feeding Gougah falls; and the falls roared at times. However, the woods around them were quiet enough so that we could almost hear each other think.

Cuong was the first to talk.

He came from a working family that had eked out at first a miserable living from their rocky ranch in the valley of Saint-Jean. Mr. and Mrs. Thao had worked hard all their life, transforming their rocky ranch into an immense truck farm. At the time of Hoang's death, they would be deemed as a well-to-do family.

We loved Cuong; Hoang loved him; but like Tan, who had never known poverty but had made of himself an outcast because of his shyness, Cuong had always been the odd man out.

He was a first lieutenant at the time, but had never left the National Military Academy. Since he graduated from it, he worked at first as an adjutant of the General Commander of the Academy, then as an instructor. For us, that meant, he continued to be in Dalat and a regular member of our group.

49

Cuong said: "We have to find out why *she* died. And if she died because of someone; I swear I will hunt that son of a bitch down and kill him without any pity."

Cuong was the most devout Christian in our group, but his talk about killing someone came out all naturally, and sounded perfectly true.

Alain said: "Why look anywhere else? Phap is the son of the bitch who killed her. I will kill him with my shotgun the next time he shows up around here."

I became uncomfortable. I said: "Look, we come to this place where we spent so many hours...and days with Hoang, to camp and to discuss until we find out with certainly who was the main cause for her suicide. Phap may or may not be the main cause. And don't deny that the four of us are at least contributing factors to this tragedy. I propose that before we go looking elsewhere, we should examine and see how one of us or all of us might have been the main cause of her death. "

The three of them glared at me angrily at first, then they looked away; then they stayed with their head hung low as if filled with guilt. Finally Tan said: "OK. Let's do that. Nam, you go first, as this is your idea."

I looked up in the sky. Massive white clouds tinged with grey sat immobile in the north and the rest of the sky was blue.

Streaks of green flitted by. I recognized the Dalat green finches darting from pine tree to pine tree. I recognized the black-throated sunbirds with long and curved beaks.

I asked: "Has any one of you slept with her?"

The three of them froze. A long and awkward silence followed. Alain exclaimed finally: "What a stupid question!"

Tan was first in a state of shock; then he managed to regain some composure. He waited until his body stopped shaking before he said: "You have no right to drag her into the mud now that she is dead. Don't you have any respect for the dead? How do you dare ask such a question?"

Trying to control his anger, Cuong asked ironically: "Have you said good-bye to sanity? Are you ripe for the madhouse?"

I followed the flight of a blue warbler with my eyes, ignoring their anger and their invectives. Finally I repeated my question: "Has any one of you slept with her?" I looked at them, one by one, calmly but insistently.

Another long silence followed. Then Cuong blurted out: "I, never."

Alain said: "Me? Not a chance!"

Tan said: "Look at poor me! No, Nam! You torture us for nothing!"

I shook my head. I said: "You are either a bunch of liars or a bunch of cowards! We will get nowhere if you do not tell the truth."

One could hear the roaring of the falls below and the song of white-cheeked laughing thrushes in the bush.

I said: "Why don't we *all* admit that we *all* had moments of intimacy with her?"

The air became heavy. The four of us could barely breathe. Alain exploded in the end; he exclaimed: "I caused her death. I am going to kill myself." Tan and Cuong shouted almost at the same time: "Me, too."

I felt as if a ton of rock sat on my chest, but I managed to say: "*Doucement!* (Take it easy!) The fact that we all had moments of intimacy with her does not mean that we were the main cause of her decision to commit suicide. Those moments may have saved her life until fourteen days ago. So let us share our secrets. Maybe by doing so we will find the key to this tragic enigma."

They all looked at me with some resentment still but were no longer in a state of revolt.

I said: "Before we do that, I want us to focus on the last two weeks she spent with us. Who heard, felt or guessed that something was wrong during those weeks. But we will do that in a little while; let us first walk around here, then sit down and have a brunch before we start talking seriously, agreed?"

I felt their relief. The three of them came and tapped me on my shoulder. They picked up their heavy knapsacks and we started walking down the slope leading into the woods. It was an easy walk as most of the vegetation consisted of pine trees. We did not mind the occasional climbing vines as all kinds of sunbirds immune to the fear of men were flitting back and forth between their bright red and shining yellow blossoms.

Alain said: "My Dad has become a birdwatcher. Since my Mom passed away, he spends most his time with his binoculars now, poor Dad. My Mom's death was devastating. For him, and for me! Now, my Dad also comes here all the time. He said that all the birds of the Lang Bian Plateau could be seen here on a sunny day."

God! Why did Alain have to mention Irene today? We could hardly handle our grief after Hoang's death. Why did Alain have to remind us of the other tragic death?

At forty-five Irene still was one of the most beautiful ladies in Dalat. She was a well-preserved older version of Hoang. If Hoang were not there, she would have been our idol.

Irene had an advantage over Hoang. She knew what she wanted. She loved Hoang with a tenderness that we tried to emulate. Irene died and part of us died with her. Irene died and Hoang mourned her almost as much as Alain and his father, feeling certainly more grief and pain than Tan, or Cuong or me.

The white clouds in the north started moving. The pine trees started singing. We remembered how great it was for us to walk around there with Hoang. Her footprints were invisible now but could be seen with our mind's eyes everywhere. The whole place had turned into sacred ground.

Tan said: "Strangely enough, another place one can see all the birds all the Lang Bian Plateau and mountains is Dalat Cemetery."

Poor Tan! Like the rest of us, he had spent hours near Irene's tomb. And now, Hoang's as well. The cemetery management had lifted some of the usual restrictions and Irene's resting place was built like a shrine. Hoang's would soon be a masterpiece of cemetery architecture.

Poor Tan! His parents, who had been married for over thirty years, suddenly split a couple of months after Irene's death. Tan turned furiously against his parents. He hated them as much as he had loved them before. While his mother wrapped herself in dignified silence his father tried to talk to him and explain to him the reasons why he had to part ways with his mother: He had somehow fallen in love with a young girl half his age and could only be happy with her. Knowing then that his father was at fault, Tan became sarcastic with him. He spent a great deal of time with his mother; but she refused to open up to him.

His father finally decided he should move out. He did; but the love nest he shared with his young mistress was only four blocks away from the family's villa.

Tan watched his mother and wondered whether she was about to explode. One day he found a revolver in his mother's bedroom and knew that things could go terribly awry for his parents.

At times he was raging mad even against us; though he never said an unkind word to Hoang.

Then one day, his ravings stopped. He walked in a daze. He would sit a little away from us, completely absorbed in his own thought. We were concerned for him then far more than when he was raving mad. Hoang did not seem to be surprised by his silence. She kept telling us: "Leave him alone! Leave him alone, please!"

*

We walked on until we reached a beautiful creek. We put our knapsacks down and sat on a rocky ledge on the bank with our bare feet in the icy cold water. The babbling of the water was soothing. There were a number of clues that had impinged upon our mind. Somehow we felt that though we might still be blindfolded by the end of the day we would know Hoang and maybe ourselves far better.

Cuong said: "I am hungry. Who wants to eat?" We didn't hear Cuong's voice but Hoang's. *That* was for many years her invitation to eat our lunch or dinner when we were together. We would immediately gather around her picnic basket and watch her pull out of it the food she had prepared. We also brought baskets full of food. But the food we ate first was always hers.

We would watch her eat. She ate with her fingers shamelessly. She seemed always to be ravenously hungry and to delight in whatever food she ate. At times she would lick her fingers when she finished and she would say: "Stop looking at me like that, bad boys!"

We too would eat with our fingers exaggerating our awkwardness while she watched and laughed: "Silly boys, look at you! No girl would accept boys with your lack of manners. You are true barbarians, sirs!"

Oh my God! We were so happy when she said that! Yes, we wanted no other girl to accept our manners.

So, Cuong had imitated *her* when he asked us to start our picnic meal. He pulled out a tin mess kit. We really wanted to kill him: the food in the tin lunch box was an imitation of the kind of food Hoang used to bring. Then we recognized the tin mess kit. It was Hoang's. She rarely brought her food in that tin mess kit, as she preferred picnic baskets. But we recognized it instantly.

Tan asked: "How come you got her mess kit?"

Cuong froze; then he said: "In 1953, about four years ago when my Mom was down with shingles for a month. Hoang would walk every day to the Saint-Jean valley where we live with this mess kit. My Mom got sicker and sicker; at moments, we thought that she would lose her eyesight. Only my Mom's left side was visibly affected; but her whole body wracked with pain for a whole month. She, who had suffered all her physical or mental pains in silence screamed at times as if she was on fire. She did not want to talk to me or my Dad; but she always welcomed Hoang's visits. And she went on eating the food Hoang brought her. Then one day, she woke up and found that most of the shingles and the pain were gone. Hoang brought her best meal to celebrate my Mom's recovery. My Mom asked whether she could keep the mess kit as a souvenir and Hoang was happy to give it to her."

I asked Cuong: "Hoang brought food to your mother every day for a month? Why you two, I mean you and Hoang, have never mentioned this?"

Cuong blushed. He looked down at the creek and said: "It's a long time ago, Nam." Then we knew that something had happened between him and Hoang four years earlier.

*

We were back to the edge of the Gougah Falls. We trembled as we knew that we had somehow sworn to tell the truth. The white clouds were now tinged with red and grey. Chased by the wind the angry clouds seemed to announce stronger wind and approaching bad weather.

But no storm, we thought, would be as violent as the one raging in our heart.

*

It was the time when Cuong, after graduation from at the National Military Academy, became an adjutant to General X. Commander of the Academy. In 1956 the Academy still had a truncated curriculum and the cadets graduated after just two years of training.

The role of an adjutant to the General gave Cuong lots of perks, and a quite flexible schedule.

56

In the summer of 1956, Cuong's mother got shingles. Few people in Vietnam knew at that time that there was such a disease. But soon enough, the inhuman pains inflicted upon the old lady were too much for Cuong and his father's to endure. Yet Cuong spent most of his afternoons with her, when his daily chores as an adjutant were finished.

He would drive his jeep past the Cathedral, to where the main street met with the sloping and graded path leading to his parents' home. He left his jeep there knowing that nobody would dare touch his military vehicle. He jumped down and rushed to his Mom's bedside. He would sit there for hours feeling the pain of his mother being transferred from her body into his. He couldn't pray. Somehow he had lost momentarily his faith. Somehow he could not believe that a loving God could punish an innocent old lady like his mother so cruelly.

Soon enough Hoang learned about Mrs. Thao's suffering. She would also drive to where Cuong left his jeep. After a while they arrived there at the same time as if the spot was the place of their appointments. They took the sloping path down to his parents' home together.

Hoang brought delicacies that she had prepared to the old lady, every day. Hoang would sit with Cuong for hours either by the bedside of Cuong's mother and cried with the old lady when the latter was awake or follow Cuong to the dim parlor and talk with him softly when his mother was asleep. In the semi darkness of the parlor, sitting on the couch Hoang would turned to Cuong, her eyes glinting with unsuppressed tears.

*

The least one could say is that the path to Saint-Jean Parish was not built with the rainy season in view. Whenever it rained, the path became muddy and slippery. Many people, including those who lived in Saint-Jean, got seriously injured in a bad fall.

One day, a big storm came. With it, came icy rain. Cuong got to the top of the slope where he parked his jeep quite early, and sat and waited for Hoang to show up. He wanted to stop Hoang there.

*

Cuong was horrified. It was the third time that Hoang slipped on the muddy slope leading to Saint-Jean.

He had tried to convince Hoang to let him bring food prepared by her to his Mom for that day; but Hoang had laughed him off. She said: "You're afraid that I will fall on this wretched road? I have no fear. Swear to me that if I fall you will carry me to your home." He read in her eyes a challenge. She said: "How many times have you carried me as we grew up?" He smiled uneasily: "More than a dozen times, I guess, but that was when we were little kids."

She was tantalizingly beautiful. She had that wicked smile on her lips. She said: "Don't worry, I am not *that* heavy! Why don't you try to carry me? Try to lift me up and walk ten steps."

He knew that she was kidding; but he did cast a look around them. There was nobody else on the road. She urged him: "Pick me up and carry me ten steps!"

He blushed profusely: "Come on, Hoang, be serious."

She looked at him until he was in total confusion; then she said: "You are strong enough to carry me from here, down the slope, then to your home, and then across the threshold. Yes, you should carry me like a bride over the threshold."

58

He was crimson. He started down the slope. She followed him; then she slipped. He caught her in time. They walked on again. But when she slipped the third time he was horrified. He said: "Give me the mess kit. Get on my back. I will carry you on my back."

She shook her head. She said: "I can hold the mess kit. I want you to carry me in your arms. I know you are strong enough to carry me to your home...and over the threshold."

With extreme care, he lifted her up. She was so light, so fragile. He carried her, trying to keep his breathing regular, and his heart from exploding. She asked: "Do you like my perfume?" He barely heard his own answer: "I love your perfume." She said: "Don't you want to kiss me?" He believed he was in a dream, so he said: "Yes, I would love to kiss you." She said: "Why don't you?" He kissed her on the cheek. She shook her head and said: "Kiss me on my lips, please." He kissed her lightly on the lips, and lost his balance. He struggled hard to recover his balance, and succeeded. She laughed and said: "Stop walking. Stay here a minute. Now kiss me like you know how." He said: "I've never kissed a girl before." Hoang smiled and said: "Kiss me again and this time, kiss me hard and I will show you how."

There was nobody else on the road.

Cuong took a deep breath and tried to calm down, then said pleadingly: "This is wrong, Hoang." She frowned. Her eyes were filled with tears. He shook his head: "It's alright that occasionally we flirt. But our flirting has always been in jest and has never gone this far. We are simply best friends, Hoang; there is a line that we should never cross."

She asked him: "You've never loved me?"

He cried out: "Yes, I have loved you all the days of my life. Like Nam, like Alain, like Tan. That's it; we all love you more than our own life. But please, I don't want to betray the others. If I kiss you hard now, I will betray them."

She said: "Don't you hear yourself talk? You're weird. I don't want you to be weird. Being with me makes you weird. I have to stop all of this nonsense. I too love the four of you more than my own life. Now, you are in great pain. Why don't you let me love you like a woman loves a man?"

Cuong said: "I don't want your pity!"

Hoang said: "No, I don't pity you. I love you. Don't tell me that you don't want right now to cross that line you just mentioned a minute ago. I don't see any line; maybe, because I've crossed it already."

Cuong stopped arguing and carried her to his parents' home. He felt guilty with his friends. He felt guilty for taking advantage of her offer. But alter all he was a young man passionately in love with her.

*

Cuong's mother was deep in sleep in her bed and so was his father, sitting in a chair next to the bed. Hoang put a finger on her lips and Cuong followed her into the dimly lit living room. She whispered: "You didn't carry me over the threshold. Now be nice and make me forgive you for failing to do that."

Outside, it poured dogs and cats again.

Inside, Cuong entered with reverence into a world that was a thousand times more promising, then more satisfying than the imaginary worlds he had dreamt about for so many years. He lost consciousness of everything except the glorious presence intimately wrapped around him—and a vague apprehension of the abyss of despair open next to him, if *or rather when* all this ended and *she w*ould no longer want to be his friend like before.

*

We knew that Cuong would not say anything further. But there were questions we wanted to ask. Tan asked after a moment: "How long did the affair last, Cuong?"

Cuong looked into the void. He said: "One month more or less. Moments of intimacy were rare though. No, Hoang was not naturally inclined to have sex. Each time we came together I felt a struggle within her. Was it her fear of sins? Was it because she felt guilty for having an affair that she had to hide from you three? I didn't know. I too was feeling guilty for hiding my affair with her from you three."

Cuong looked at us now, he said: "We tried to make up to you by spending time with you more than before; because we felt like we had committed an indiscretion or even adultery by doing what we did. Yet it was heavenly to be intimate with her. One day, after I dozed off, I woke up to find her standing at the window crying. I asked her: "Why do you cry." She shook her head violently making her lustrous hair swirl around her. I came closer and put my hand on her shoulder. She turned around and said softly: "*I cried because I've found that a man can make love to a woman gently, selflessly.*" I did not understand what she meant by that. Somehow what she said sent a sharp pain through my mind. I said: "Even the most evil man would be gentle with you Hoang! Even the most callous man would make love to you worshipfully." She stared at me then shuddered and started sobbing uncontrollably: "Are you sure of that, Cuong?" In her eyes I read despair and horror, then relief. I held her tightly a long time waiting for her to calm

61

down. Eventually her sobbing subsided. She held my face with both hands and kissed me on my closed eyes and said: "You reconcile me with the world, Cuong! Thank you, thank you!" Oh my God, why did she have to thank me? Didn't she see that a minute with her was an eternity of happiness for me?"

His head hanged low when he added: "Somehow I knew that day that she was about to end our affair.

*

"I still remembered the day as if it were yesterday." Cuong said grimly. "That day, I had the premonition that something was about to happen. I had never believed that our love affair would last forever, sure. But it was a shock all the same when Hoang said, calmly but firmly: "We should stop seeing each other like this, Cuong." I trembled and waited for the other shoe to drop. I already heard her words in my mind: "We should stop seeing each other after this." But Hoang said: "Let's go back to being friends like we were before this." Relief, then savage joy overwhelmed me. I was in tears. I said: "As long as I can see you as a friend I will never be unhappy." I hugged her and she hugged me. Then both of us started laughing insanely. That's it. That's how it began and how it ended."

Tan said pensively: "Yet, there was no real beginning, and there was no real end; don't you agree?"

Cuong nodded silently. We sat there, waiting for the rainstorm to arrive. But, we knew it would only reach Gougah Falls in a couple of hours. Still we sat without exchanging a word. How many times we had sat like that with Hoang, contemplating the sky, feeling happy, and lazy, feeling like we owned the world. After a long while I suggested: "Alain, it's your turn. Please, tell us your story."

*

It took Alain a moment to put his thoughts and recollections in order. Alain was the least romantic guy among us. He was a matter-of fact, down-to-earth boy since childhood. He was never lyrical. And we loved him for that.

Irene, his mother, on the other hand, was pure poetry. All her life was pure poetry. It was not because she wanted to escape from the miasma of her husband's obsessive sense of guilt (Dr. Mirot practically killed two Vietnamese women, his patients, when he was very young and very irresponsible). No, Irene did not share his sense of guilt. She would like to see Alain, her son, grow up to become a poet. But as soon as he could spell, Alain started correcting her whenever she said something unrealistic. As soon as he could count, Alain loved to put numbers in a string. He was soon knowledgeable enough to check the ledgers of Dr. Mirot's plantations.

As he hated leaving Dalat for any stretch of time he became at the age of twenty-five the general manager of all the tea, coffee and rubber plantations of his family. His professional career made him even tougher in dealing with people, except with us. We were the only ones who could make him recite Verlaine's poems or marvel at *Kim Vân Kiều* lines. But the real chink in his armor was Hoang. Through that chink, she could get in and turn him into a wreck, or make of him the happiest man on earth, at any time. He knew it, but he did not mind.

If he worshipped Hoang, he loved his mother with a passion that we all understood, as we too, loved her beyond reason.

Then one day in 1957 Irene died.

*

Alain suffered like a dog. He walked around like a zombie. He felt as if half of his chest had been blown away leaving a big hole where his heart had been. His head ached. How could breast cancer kill so fast? Two weeks earlier, Irene told Dr. Mirot that she felt sick. He found lumps in her left breast. They flew to Saigon the next day and Irene was left in the able hands of French doctors at the Grall Hospital. Dr. Mirot flew back to Dalat and assured Alain that his Mom had a few lumps and that the doctors at Grall would take care of them. "No sweat!" he said.

Yet for the next few days Alain was on a rollercoaster. The news from Saigon was not good, then fairly good, then good, then back to fairly good, then bad. Then devastating!

It was cancer all right. Was it first stage, second stage? Was it third stage? Has it metastasized? Yes, it has.

"How long does she have?"

"She may have a couple of weeks ... or days!"

Irene wanted to be flown back to Dalat to die there.

They flew her back to Dalat. We surrounded her with our love; but knowing with wretched certainty that she was going to die made our days and nights a long and horrendous agony. On the last day we watched her breathe with more and more difficulty. We looked at one another with distress for a second. When we turned to her again we saw that she had stopped breathing.

Alain did not remember how he could survive the placing of Irene's body in the coffin; or his kissing her a last time before her coffin was rolled into the Cathedral; or his Dad's lachrymose eulogy. He only remembered that part of his life was buried when the coffin, with Irene inside, was lowered down into the excavated ground.

He remembered standing there feeling all the emptiness inside. He remembered the pain and the numbness that came after he went past the pain threshold.

He remembered seeing us, standing in a group, pretending to be brave.

We followed him to his home after the burial. We went upstairs and shut ourselves in Irene's room. After a while, Tan and Cuong went downstairs and brought back four or five bottles of hard liquor. We sat there and drank one cup after another. Alain did not say anything. So, we drank in silence. Hoang kept up with our drinking, emptying one cup after another. She looked stunning; her large eyes brimming with tears. We did not know what would or could happen next. We did not know how that drinking bout would end; but we did not care to know.

It was Dr. Mirot who came and pulled us out of there. He drove us home, making two short stops to let Tan and Cuong out near their home; then drove on as if he did not have a destination. Finally he stopped his car at the roadside and said to Hoang, who sat in the front seat: "Whether Alain could retain his sanity or not will depend in a large measure on the four of you; and especially you, Hoang." Neither Hoang nor I said anything. After a while, Hoang asked: "What's Alain's plan for the immediate future?"

Dr. Mirot said: "He plans to leave for our Terre Rouge coffee plantation early tomorrow. He said he couldn't stay in our house anymore."

*

Before Irene died she called us into her bed room. She said gently: "Alain, my son, please, wait outside a moment. You will come in when I've finished with your friends."

Alain stepped outside and we came close to her. Irene took Hoang's hand in hers. She cried a little then said: "For thirty years I have lived with a man whose sense of guilt banished almost everything from his inner life. He also banished the outside world likewise. I had no access to him. I felt abandoned and I needed tenderness and love. So, I had a few liaisons over the years. Each and every one of them proved to be a disappointment. May God forgive me for my weakness! My poor husband suspected what was going on and suffered tremendously from my infidelities. They added more to his sense of guilt. And I was further shut out of his life. It has been a vicious circle. And we haven't found an exit until now. I have asked my husband not to bury me in a Catholic cemetery. I will be all right in the municipal cemetery. I want you to listen to me carefully now: You are in a similar vicious circle yourselves. Hoang, you have to have the courage *to forgive the person or persons* who hurt you so badly that you had to surround yourself with friends who act like the walls of a fortress around you. The five of you have been spell-bound for so many years that *you can no longer imagine a normal life;* Hoang, you have to release the boys, to allow them to lead a life without being bound to you and to each other to this point."

Hoang put her head on Irene's hand and cried softly. The three of us, standing there did not understand the meaning of Irene's last wish. We stood there watching hopelessly the two women we have loved most in life cry.

After a while Irene said: "All of you please kiss me one more time. On your way out, please ask Alain to come in."

That was the last time we heard Irene's voice.

We did come back to see her once more. But she could no longer talk. Then, she passed away.

*

Early in the morning when Dalat was still wrapped in a sea of mist and fog Alain started driving to "Parfum de Rêve" (Scent of a Dream), the manicured coffee plantation at Terre Rouge, that he had dedicated to his mother after he was named director general of his family's plantations. He had no definite plans. His whole body was aching and he longed for the sight of bougainvilleas around the plantation and around the white villa where he had been spending his time whenever he came and worked at Terre Rouge.

In the villa he would find his Winchester M94 hunting rifle and his Mossberg 935 shotgun. He had a vague idea that he would go deer hunting the next morning. He toyed for a short moment with the idea of arranging for a hunting accident. But he shook his head: "Mom is dead, but Hoang is still here; Tan, Cuong and Nam are still here. I suffer like a dog, but I cannot go out and commit suicide. Dalat and my friends will nurse me back to life; even though I will be walking around with half of my chest blown away and with a gaping hole where my heart was."

Ashamed for having lapsed mentally into grandiloquent expressions, Alain stepped with rage on the break and his Citroën DS screamed and stopped instantaneously in front of his white villa. Stepping down from the car, he noticed Hoang's car parked inconspicuously under the bougainvilleas at the far side of the fence.

Swinging his small suitcase over his shoulder, he wondered what Hoang was doing in his plantation at that early time of the day. He thought that she had come with Tan, Cuong and me. He promised to himself another evening of booze with us like the night before.

He was surprised to find Hoang by herself. She was sitting in the living room turning the pages of a magazine absentmindedly. Alain announced his presence by clearing his throat. Hoang got up and explained, "Chi Ba let me in and made coffee for me. Perfume of Dream Coffee is quite extraordinary!"

Alain noted that Hoang had turned crimson when she saw him. He asked without thinking: "What are you doing here?" She pouted: "You mean I am not welcome here? OK. I am going. You don't have to show me the way out."

He put the suitcase down and instinctively opened wide his arms as if trying to prevent her from getting away: "No, Ma'am, you are not going anywhere." He staggered back a couple of small steps as she threw herself unexpectedly on him. To regain his balance he had to hold her tightly. He felt her body tremble as she sobbed. He held her more tightly. From her body a healing flow of warmth seemed to have found its way through his body and his soul. He wondered whether he was dreaming. Then, her lips were all over his neck, his cheeks, his forehead and his lips. He said: "Slow down, Hoang; let me think! Give me a second to think!"

She laughed him off with tears still streaming down from her eyes: "Too late to think now." She kissed him again and again until he became breathless. It was with great difficulty that he escaped from her arms. He said:" Look, Hoang. Don't let your compassion or pity make you do things that you will live to regret. You don't love me. I mean you have loved me always as a friend; and your loving friendship has made me happy all these years. But you don't love me as a woman loves a man. Don't do this to yourself. Don't do this to me!"

She wiped her eyes with her sleeve like when she was a kid and looked at him until he was in total confusion. She asked softly: "So, you don't love me like a man loves a woman? You have never wanted me? Never wanted to hold me? Say it then! Say: "I have never ever loved you. I have never ever wanted to hold you, Hoang!" And I will be gone in a minute."

Alain walked over to the sofa, sat down and covered his face with his hands. Hoang came and sat down next to him. Soon enough, Alain felt the weight of her head on his lap. His body and his brain screamed in unison: "This is pure folly!" But there was no going back. He knew that. He also knew that he had been waiting for years, for this or something like this to take place. He also knew that if he did not make love to her right away, he would live to regret this miracle that could happen only once in a lifetime.

For the first time in his life, the unreasonable was the only option. For the first time, he let his heart and his senses take precedence over his brain. He was drowned in the scent of her body and buried under her kisses. He picked her up and carried her upstairs to his bedroom, his lair that had never admitted another female presence.

*

A pattern was shown. Hoang had come to Cuong and Alain when they suffered the most. All of us recognized that pattern now. We looked at Tan and he looked away. Did she come to him when he suffered the most? For example when his parents split, a few months after Irene died?

I asked Alain: "How long did your affair last?" Alain was surprised that I had to ask. He said "One month, exactly like with Cuong?"

Tan threw up his hands: "Yes, of course, it must last one month."

Another pattern: the affairs ended after a month.

Cuong asked Alain: "Is there anything else you think you should tell us about the affair?"

Alain cast a quick glance on each one of us before he said, addressing Cuong especially: "You should know as much as I do that during all the weeks and days of the affair, I was feeling that I did not deserve so much happiness and fearing that in the end Hoang would not want me any longer as a friend. Then, oh how much relief I felt when she said after breaking up with me: "Let us be friends like before!" To be her friend again while knowing that she had given me everything she could give was more than heavenly. Though she put an end to the affair, she did not say that it would never happen again. In the meantime, I was to enjoy being with her, being very close to her, like I had been since our childhood. Though I still mourned for my Mom, I was no longer walking around with half of my chest blown off. Hoang was divine. She gave me back the world, my friends."

Cuong nodded agreement. I asked: "How often did you meet intimately?"

Alain, the kid who was good with the numbers said immediately: "In all, seven times. Like Cuong said, Hoang was not looking for fun or pleasure. Moments of intimacy seemed to make her feel uneasy. Sometimes they made her cry. When she first came to me, she wanted to heal me, to reduce my pain, to make me accept the passing of my Mom. One day she looked at me for a long time and said: "Before your Mom died, she told me to set you free, all the four of you. She said that the five of us formed an unholy and weird circle. The circle would not allow us to have a normal life. I had to come to you like an ordinary woman to break the spell, to say: "See, I am just a woman!" I told her that she was not just a woman; that holding her was like holding a celestial lady, an angel!"

Tan nodded agreement: "She was like a goddess of compassion." It was strange that Tan should use such an expression as he was a devoted Buddhist, and what he said could be twisted into a verbal sacrilege.

But he looked at us as if he challenged us to contradict him. We didn't contradict him.

I asked Alain: "Did she cry at any time during that month, when she was with you? " Alain nodded: "One day I found her walking along the fences of my villa under the blossoming bougainvilleas. I was about to walk up to her when I noticed that she was crying. I waited for her to come back to the villa and asked her: "I saw you cry while you were walking outside. Are you regretting already that we've had gone into this folly?"

She blushed and said: "God be my witness! I haven't regretted nor will I ever regret that we've had these few weeks together. I cried because you are so good to me, so gentle, so generous during our moments of intimacy." I still cannot understand why she said what she said. "Alain frowned and mused aloud: "Unless someone had hurt her grievously. But that's absurd. We had been around her constantly since she's eight. Who could've hurt her? "

We looked at each other and nodded agreement. We had served as a defensive wall around her all those years; how could anyone hurt her without our knowledge?

71

After a moment I suggested: "It's your turn, Tan, tell us your story!"

*

The rain clouds had now invaded more than half of the sky. Tan who had been leaning comfortably against a pine tree, sat straight up. He said: "If Hoang did not arrive on the scene at the right moment, my Mom would have shot my Dad dead, that day."

He got our full attention. Neither he nor Hoang had mentioned that near-tragedy before. Of course we knew that his father, Dr. Thieu, had met a young girl half his age and sued for divorce in order to marry her. We all watched helplessly as Tan raged against his Dad.

We were amazed when suddenly his rage was gone overnight.

Now, we could guess what had happened and why when we tried to ask Tan the reasons for his dazed look and strange silence, Hoang would say: "Leave him alone, please."

*

"At that time, my Dad had left our home. He lived openly with Lien, his young mistress in a house four blocks away from us. Living in the old family home full of memories of happier days was a torture for me; I am sure it was worse for my Mom. Then one evening Mom said: "Let's go pay a courtesy visit to your Dad." The glint in her eyes should have warned me that she was not going there to be pleasant or courteous. But I was so much in pain that I did not give enough attention to anything. I got into the car, and my Mom drove like a mad woman. I didn't care to tell her to slow down. "

"When we arrived at my Dad's love nest," Tan went on, "my Mom was too fast for me. She got out of the car, burst into the living room, took her revolver out of her handbag and could have killed my Dad right away; but she seemed to hesitate between two targets: my Dad and Lien. That minute of hesitation saved my Dad's life. I was at the door frozen on my track, unable to move a muscle. But a side door opened and Hoang appeared. Without thinking about the danger to herself, she ran to my Dad and covered him with her body. She also extended her hand to cover Lien's face.

"Stunned, my Mom dropped the gun and ran out of my Dad's house. I did not even look at my Dad and Lien; I took Hoang's hand and asked: "Why are you here?"

Hoang said: "I came to see you at your Mom's house; then I saw the two of you get into a car. I followed you here. When you and your Mom got out of the car, I saw her rage and I ran to the side door hoping I arrived in time to give your Dad a warning. But your Mom burst into the house and she took a revolver out of her handbag in a flash. I did not have the time to think, that was why I jumped and landed between your Mom and your Dad."

"I looked at my Dad. I looked at him, up and down, and said: "You should be ashamed of yourself." Then I left."

"When I came out of the house, my Mom was long gone with our car. Hoang said: "Come with me. Let me give you a ride." She drove me to my empty office that occupied a large corner of our pharmacy. That office was at the time my refuge. I worked at that office fourteen hours a day, dreading to go home and spend the evening with my Mom. After a while, I even stopped going home. After I finished working for the day,

73

and after all my employees had all gone, I ascended the stairs and went up to my apartment upstairs, ate some biscuits, got myself drunk and went to bed."

"I did not know what was worse: Going back to Mom's home and seeing her mope around in silence or staying alone at my apartment above my office and getting drunk. "

"That night, Hoang cast a quick glance at my cluttered desk then at the clock on the wall and decreed: "It's already seven. We can still go out for dinner, of course. But I guess, you have no wish to dine out tonight. So let's go upstairs. I will cook you a good meal."

"The suggestion that she would stay and cook a meal for me sounded like a hint at intimacy. I looked at her with gratitude. She saw my eyes and laughed: "You silly boy! Don't you see that the dice is cast, and that tonight I will stop being merely a friend?" My hearts missed quite a few beats. I protested while my heart was about to burst with savage joy: "Hoang, you don't have to..." She laughed again: "Tell you what! Let's have a few drinks first. Don't worry! Even drunk I still can cook a decent meal. After dinner we will have a few more drinks. Then, you will stop being shy. Is that a good plan?"

*

"Even after all the wines and the digestive liquors I was still more than aware of my inadequacies, of the immense distance between Hoang and me. She still was an ethereal presence, a celestial being and I still was an awkward earthly creature. I didn't kiss her back when kissed; I didn't dare touch the buttons on her dress when she had yanked my shirt open.

"Like you all I had revered her and worshipped her. I was horrified at the thought that I would disappoint her one way or another. But she managed to create confidence, to draw me little by little into a game of tender responses and to break down all my feeble defenses."

"I wanted to scream at moments: "This is too much! This is inconceivable." The night advanced and I fell asleep. In the morning I woke up and was really surprised to find her still in my bed. She had not faded away like a dream. I marveled that she was still there by my side. "

He stopped then said, as if Hoang was in front of him: "Oh, why did you commit suicide, Hoang? It must be me who killed you! I've killed you with my inadequacies and my stupid shyness."

He cried like a child now, brushing his tears and his nose with his sleeve.

I asked:" How long did it last, Tan?"

We were not surprised by his answer: "One month, thirty lifetimes. Thirty lifetimes of bliss, undeserved, outrageous bliss! Yes, over that month we might have been intimate five or six times, but that was more than enough", he said.

Alain asked: "What did Hoang say when she broke up with you?" Tan smiled sadly now: "There was no real break up! She simply said:" Let's stop going to bed together. Let's be friends like before." No, I didn't feel any pain when that episode came to an end."

Their eyes were all turned to me now. It's my turn, I knew.

*

The rain clouds hanged very low now. A chilly wind ran from pine tree to pine tree. We knew it was time to set up our tent. We had tents that could hold well to far stormier winds. It took us a few minutes to put up the tent and get in.

As we set up the tent I remembered vividly how we started camping with Hoang as kids; how she cracked up laughing when our six-man tent was blown flat under sustained wind. How we crawled out of the tent, ran to the nearest bush and kept talking far into the night and fell asleep. The time of our innocence!

Even at that time we noticed Hoang's obvious independence. Her parents never said anything to us when we disappeared with her into the woods for days in a row.

Later, when we were fourteen and fifteen we were more careful not to touch her more than necessary when she had some difficulty climbing a rock, not to brush against her when in a narrow passage, not to look too intently at her when she blushed.

There were special moments when we had to hug her like on Christmas Eve or New Year. But we did that like the most loyal subjects hugging a radiant sovereign who had just bestowed on them the highest nobility title.

We were not immune from the jeering and badmouthing of others. Some called us Queen Bee and her Four Drones. As long as Hoang didn't care we just ignored the taunting. But if Hoang got mad, the five of us would start a fight and go at it with everything we got until the guy or guys cried uncle.

We had to set up the tent in a hurry, but we knew that with Hoang we had mastered the skills of tent setting. We made ourselves comfortable under the tent as the storm came upon us. We knew that the tent would hold well to rain and winds.

*

"Apparently the three of you had moments of intimacy with her long before she came to me." I said.

"How do you know?" Alain asked.

I said: "Cuong's Mom got shingles in the summer of 1956; your mother, Alain, died in 1957; and Tan's parents separated in the same year. Hoang came to me in late 1958 after she was engaged to Phap."

"One day, on a stormy afternoon, after I finished a lecture on Zhuangzi at the newly founded Dalat University, I went home and found Hoang in my living room. For the first time I saw Hoang act embarrassed. I joked, with some bitterness: "Phap, your fiancé, would be mad if he learns about this." I said that as a lame joke. But the joke made both of us even less comfortable. Hoang, who had blushed when I came in, turned crimson now. She stood there watching me as if she tried to read my thoughts."

"Then she took the plunge. She said firmly: "I want to spend the night with you? Do you object?"

"Sudden anger overwhelmed me and for the first time I screamed at her: "Damn you Hoang! Why do you have to have to make that kind of joke to me now? We, I mean Alain, and Tan and Cuong and I have suffered like hell when you announced that you would get married with Phap, a guy whom we didn't know from Adam. Do you know that even now we do not know whether we should go to Saigon and shoot your Phap dead or go out and kill ourselves?"

My first reaction stunned her. My vehemence seemed to open suddenly her eyes to our pain. She ran at me and wrapping herself around me she said: "I did not make a joke, Nam. This is no joke, please, believe me. If you want, I will break up with Phap, I will cancel the planned marriage. Love me, Nam. Don't push me away."

*

Alain remarked almost accusingly: "So, your affair did not begin like ours! She was in love with you! She did not come to you like a goddess of compassion who came to a leper. She did not come to you because you were suffering..."

I shook my head. I had to disagree: "Remember that at that time all and every one of us suffered like hell!"

Cuong said: "But she came to you alone; she did not come to us. She was ready to scrap her marriage plans for you!"

Outside, the storm had turned more violent. We listened to the thunder and the gurgling of water streaming down in rivulets around the tent into Gougah waterfalls.

Yes, it was a stormy evening like this, when in my apartment I felt how vital for me to have Hoang's body pressed against mine, even if it were for a minute only.

I said: "Hoang, please, think hard about the situation. Phap is a wealthy and famous doctor. He will be able to offer you the moon...and the stars. Look at me! I am an assistant professor of Eastern philosophy with only two books under my name..."

Hoang started kissing me like crazy. Between kisses, she laughed and said: "So you think that I need more wealth?

No, Nam, I have been brought up a rich kid. My Dad's sawmill and lumber business have always provided us with more money than we could spend. No, I wanted to be married to Phap, and get away far from you four, because I could not make up my mind to choose one among you. That was why I wanted to get away from you all, to forget all about you, in order to have an ordinary, a normal life. That is, until today, until now, until this very minute. I suddenly realize that I have been in love with you all these years. I choose you, Nam. I know I will have a normal life with you. Phap has disappeared from my life as if he had never existed."

I said: "I know that there are thousands of reasons why I shouldn't let you stay here tonight. But with you hugging me like this I cannot think. Please let go of me a moment and let's discuss this seriously."

"She released me and took a few steps back. But I couldn't think. I was drifting between a man dreaming of being a butterfly and a butterfly dreaming of being a man. She was a dream within a dream, an evolving dream that filled the room, the building then the storm outside and the whole universe."

"I sat down defeated. She came and sat next to me and asked: "Tell me just one reason why I shouldn't stay here tonight, and all the remaining nights of our lives to fulfill all your wildest dreams of joy and happiness?"

I said lamely: "I've forgotten all the thousands of reasons why we shouldn't become lovers. Now I only see the reasons why we should be together for all eternity."

She clapped her hands and laughed and stood up and danced around me like an overjoyed little girl.

Then she was no longer a little girl. She came and sat on my thighs, put her lips on mine, and said: "Let's start our new life together."

I was the butterfly that had stopped dreaming to be a man. I was a man who was a butterfly.

*

"Why and how did it end?" Alain wanted to know.

"It was a month later. She again waited in my apartment for me to come back in the evening. When I came in I noticed immediately that she was no longer happy. I asked her: "What happened?"

"She came over to me and I knew she had been crying for hours. She said: "Hold me tight so that I can ask you this question." "What question?" I asked."

" When we are already married, suppose Alain or Cuong or Tan suffers a great deal, suppose one of them goes through a hellish tragedy of some sort, and I offer myself to him; would that give you a lot of pain?"

"I felt as if the world was turning upside down. I held her for a long time without saying anything. She urged me: "Tell me how you would handle that?" I shook my head: "I don't know! I don't really know."

"I saw the enormity of the question. I asked her: "You want to ask me whether I would be a complaisant husband? I know that we have been a bunch of weird children. We have played "Virgin Queen Bee and the Four Drones" for so many years that your question sounds legitimate somewhat. But marriage puts us squarely into the world of adults and in that world there is no room for Queen Bee and the Four Drones. What you want me to do is to embrace polyandry."

"I waved my hands as if I were telling a joke. But I knew that the question was deadly serious. Alain, Tan and Cuong were more than brothers to me. I was prepared to die for them at any time. Hoang loved them no less than I loved them. If they were hurt badly and she slept with them to make their pain go away, how could I blame her?"

"I felt tired. I told her: "I know you love them...""

"She said: "Yes, I love them almost as much as I love you. The four of you make the world a wonderful place for me to live in. And more than that, without the four of you, *I would have killed myself a long time ago.*" The last part of her remark was obviously a slip to tongue. She paled as soon as she uttered the words. "

"From somewhere in my unconscious a question surged to my lips: *"Why would you kill yourself a long time ago?"*

"She stared blankly at me a moment then turned away."

"I said hastily: "I really don't care, Hoang. Do whatever you want. You are free to do whatever you want. I will not feel much pain if one day you share your bed with Alain or Tan, or Cuong.""

"She burst into tears. She said: "No, I will never do that to you. I prefer to die rather than to hurt your feelings.""

"She ran out of the apartment, rushed to her car in the storm. I was afraid that she could get killed driving in that kind of weather. "

"She never came back. A month later, she was married to Phap."

*

Alain said: "You blew it, Nam. You were given the best chance to pull her out of there; but you didn't do nearly enough. You killed her!" I looked at him. Oh, I hoped he was right. I hoped that her suicide was the result of my mishandling the last evening of our affair; because if that was proven to be true, my torment would end, my quest for the ultimate reason for her tragic death would be over. Alain suddenly grabbed my arm and said: "I am sorry, I shouldn't blame you; it was me who killed her."

Cuong said: "We all blew it. We together with Phap, her husband, we all blew it and we all killed her." His verdict might be correct, but it was not convincing enough. Our Gougah trip didn't put an end to our search for answer.

We spent a sleepless night in the tent, first drinking coffee, then vodka and whisky, listening to the roar of the storm that lasted until dawn. The storm outside was nothing compared with the storm inside our soul. We stared at the darkness inside us and found no key to the enigma that gnawed ravenously at our heart.

Somehow the trip and the "wake" did clarify a few things between Hoang and us. We wondered where she had found the energy, the faith and the compassion to pour on us so many blessings, to introduce us to so many parts of paradise. Did she find it in her family, her mother and her father, her Catholicism? We shook our heads. No, her parents were the coldest couples in our midst. They seemed to have dried up inside. They couldn't be the source of Hoang's selflessness and her inexhaustible capacity for giving. And Hoang's Catholicism seemed to have shrunk gradually as she grew up.

She never mentioned sin, church, redemption, charity or hope. She seemed to be barricading herself against all intrusion of faith into her life.

*

The revelation came at the low-key ceremony marking the completion of the first month of Hoang's passing.

The living room of her parents was, as always, uninviting. Hoang's father mumbled formal thanks for our presence. Her mother looked at us vacantly. It was Phap who broke the ice. He had brought with him an enormous and heavy canvas tote bag. He opened it. The bag was full of bottles of spirits, liquors and wines. He said: "Let's get drunk."

His insane behavior made us laugh and in a minute he succeeded in befriending us. Hoang's parents were scandalized but because they were playing hosts they had to smile and bear it. We found glasses and an ice bucket quickly and Phap filled the glasses to the brim with whisky. We burst out laughing. He was obviously challenging Hoang's parents and contriving to make them mad.

Alain raised his glass and said: "To Hoang!"

We, including Phap, raised our glasses and said in unison: "To Hoang."

Hoang's father managed to say: "We are sorry, but we don't drink."

We let that pass and focused on emptying our glasses.

Unexpectedly Phap said: "My friends, let's find out why Hoang committed suicide. Let's do that before we get really drunk."

We froze. Then we looked at him. He stared vacantly at a wall, his face twisted and contorted with a succession of violent emotions: anger, despair, sorrow, bewilderment and guilt. We recognized him at once as one of us. Pained beyond endurance we were far better off than him because the four of us could share that pain among us. He was alone. He was by himself. He must have been in hell since Hoang died.

I said: "Look, Phap! We have since she died tried to piece up together all the information available to determine why she died. But we have come out of those exercises empty handed."

Phap looked up then asked us with tears in his eyes: "Did any one of you sleep with her in the two weeks she spent with you before she committed suicide?"

Tan said: "None of us. No, Hoang would never betray you; she would never betray her word."

Phap asked in a monotone: "Yet she did sleep with every one of you at least once before she got married to me, right?"

I said: "Yes."

Phap asked again: "Do you think she was a slut?"

Cuong said with controlled anger: "Phap, we understand and share your pain. But please never hint at such a thing. She was an angel of compassion. She came to us only when we were broken, when we were hurt beyond endurance. She never thought of herself whenever she became intimate with us."

Alain, and I and Tan nodded agreement. Phap looked at us for a long while then he burst into tears again. He cried like a man would cry, without shame. Then, wiping his face with his handkerchief and clearing his voice he said:" The one who pushed her to suicide must be here in this room. Who is he then?"

He stopped a moment then commented as if to himself: "The four of you, my friends, would die a thousand deaths rather than hurt her. So, how could you push her to suicide? Hoang never told me about her affairs with you; but she said enough to help me guess right. Yes, when she died I understood almost everything. I knew that you made life acceptable to her. I understood that without you she would have died a long time ago. No, you could not be the cause of her death. How about me? Oh my God! I loved her more than my own life, so how could I push her to suicide?"

We felt defeated. The mystery remained a mystery.

In the silence that followed Phap asked nonsensically: "When did the five of you become inseparable? When you were nine, ten or eleven?"

Cuong said: "She tagged along with us since we were eight or nine. Then when she was ten, she disappeared from the scene. When she came back she was depressed for a while. Then we became inseparable."

He looked at us as if asking for confirmation. Alain, Tan and I nodded.

Unexpectedly, Phap stood up and emitted a long and savage howl. He looked completely insane now. He went to the coat rack near the door, took his overcoat that was hung there and pulled a gun out of the coat pocket.

He came back to his seat and pointing his gun at Hoang's father he asked articulating every word as if to make sure that the old man understood his question: "Did you molest her when she was ten?"

We were petrified and devastated. How could Phap make an accusation of such gravity without any apparent reason? On what ground did he make his horrendous accusation? We turned our eyes on Hoang's father and were horrified. His face was ashen and not only his hands but his whole body too was wracked with pain and guilt and fear. We now remembered the hints that she had given us: *without the four of you I would have killed myself a long time ago;* then her thanking us for being gentle and selfless with her; thanking us for being generous with her. Oh, my God, Why didn't we understand at the time?

Hoang's mother continued to look past us; her vacant eyes remained vacant like they had always been before.

Phap asked again, this time he shouted his question: "Did you rape her when she was ten?"

The question acted like a hammer. We saw it fly at Hoang's father and strike him across his chest. His body sagged visibly. Phap came over and stood a foot from him and said: "I'm going to kill you, monster. I know that they will hand me a life sentence for this. But I don't really care."

Surprisingly, Hoang's father stood up and discarded the gun muzzle away gently and said: "If I am to die, I will die by my own hand. You still have a long life to live. Don't waste it." Ignoring Phap as if he were not there, the old man walked to a cabinet at the far end of the living room. He took a key that hanged on a rope chain that he had been wearing around his neck. We guessed that the drawer he tried to open should contain a gun. But he couldn't open the drawer. He screamed: "Open up, damn it", yanking vainly at the heavy drawer.

Hoang's mother had a sad smile. She shook her head and said: "I changed the lock. I knew some day you would want to use the gun in it."

She became alive and tears ran down her cheeks as she said: "After I changed the lock, I threw the key into the Great Lake. Hoang knew that there was a gun in the drawer. She attempted many times to open it, but couldn't."

I walked over to Phap and took the gun away from him. I said: "They have suffered enough for the crime." Phap glared at me for a moment then he said: "You may be half right. They still have many more years to suffer for the crime."

I said to Phap: "Hoang once blurted out: "Without the four of you I would have killed myself a long time ago."

Hoang's mother swallowed hard then said: "That's absolutely true. She ran away from this house; she fled this world and found a shelter in the four of you. That's why I did not say anything when she disappeared with you for days in the woods. Then one day she came to me and cried like a baby. She said she couldn't go on using you selfishly like that any longer. She said she had to release you, to break the spell that bound you to her. She wanted you to have normal families and normal lives. She said she would go out and find the first man who wanted to marry her and take her away from here."

She looked at Phap and said: "Fortunately she got you. It's like having a blind date and found the perfect man. She opened herself to you. Whatever she could not tell you, she made you guess. Within two years with her you knew her more than her friends of over twenty years. But she couldn't be separated from them forever. She couldn't be separated from them for long. She had to come back. She had to come back and die. She thought that maybe only her death would break that spell they were living under."

We had goose bumps when she went on with a cavernous voice: "Do you want to know what happened to her when she was ten?"

All of us said in unison: "No, absolutely not."

She stared at us uncomprehendingly, then after a long while she asked: "Are you afraid of the truth? Are you afraid to look at her wounds? Are you afraid of seeing how an innocent, confident, happy child feels when she is suddenly robbed of her childhood and youth, her innocence, her joy and her hope, her faith in God and men, flayed alive and thrown into hellfire to burn day and night, by her own father?"

I was about to explode. I really wanted to tell her and her husband: "If you two need to confess, please go to the confessional or a tribunal, find a priest or a judge."

But instead I turned to my friends and said softly: "Let's get out of here; let's go, my friends."

We did not know that Hoang's mother could be that fast. She was already at the door barring our exit with her extended arms and with the fire in her eyes. She was ignoring our objections. She screamed: "You've got to know what happened to her. You cannot run away from the truth. She was the apple of her father's eye; and she was so happy that he loved her so much. She accompanied him on trips deep into the forest. He went there to identify rare wood trees and talk with lumberjacks. Our lumber business was expanding very fast and he needed to negotiate with loggers, transporters, contractors. At times, he took the time out and went hunting with her. Then, oh my God, one day when Hoang was ten, he came back with her. I knew something was wrong immediately. I asked: "Why is Hoang so pale and so sick? " He said: "I was stupid enough to kill a deer in front of her; isn't true, darling?" Hoang sobbed while she said: "Yes, Mom, he killed a deer in front of me." I asked: "Where is the deer?" He said: "I gave it away." After that, she never accepted to go with her father again. She spent all her time crying whenever she thought I was not looking. Little by little, I put two and two together. One day, I decided to confront him. I waited until both he and Hoang were in front of me, then I screamed at him: "Did you molest her the last time she went with you?" Hoang, shaken out of her lethargy also screamed: "Yes, Mom, he raped me."

There was no way to stop her now. Horrified as we were we had to stay there and listen.

She went on: "I blessed the day she went back and hanged around with you. But I knew she was hurt beyond healing, or rather she was dead inside. She saw herself as a broken doll, a dried up fountain. She saw herself condemned to a life without joy, without hope, always ashamed of herself and always feeling dishonored, sullied. She did not look for redemption in this life or in the afterworld. She lived in hell literally."

"She found some solace with you four; but only up to a point. She had to have you around her and knowing that it was selfish to take you away from all the other classmates, and young people your age. She knew that she was taking advantage of you. But she could not see how she would be able to survive without you."

"I knew later on, many years later that she had short term affairs with each one of you. She came to you when you suffered the most, not out of compassion but because she couldn't stand seeing you hurt. However, each time she was intimate with one of you she was forced to relive the horror of her rape. That drove her crazy; that forced her to break up quickly."

89

"She thought that by marrying Phap she would be able to live a normal life. But she could not lead a normal life. How could she live a normal life when she was always in hell?"

She stopped then shouted: "You can go now. Leave us here to burn in hell, this life and the next."

*

There are five of us again. We are inseparable. Phap moved his practice to Dalat and took the place of his wife in our group. We still are the weird five. We spend inordinate time to revisit the places where Hoang used to be. But there are no Queen Bee and her Drones anymore. We form a circle around an absence. We are the five planets circling around a fixed star that is no longer there.

Only when we sit around her tomb our circle has a center. We love her beyond space, and time, and eternity.

We told her: "You are no longer an angel with broken wings. You have flown back to God who can heal anything and who has kept ready for you one of his best mansions."

And we know that from where she is, she cannot help seeing how much we love her and miss her.

Andre Nguyen Van Chau

THE SWORD AND THE WOODEN FISH

THE SWORD

The Sword and the Wooden Fish is based on a period of Vietnam's history loosely called by historians as "the period of North and South Rulers" (Nam Bắc Triều), when the North was ruled by the Trinh Lords who usurped all the power of the totally overshadowed Kings of the Restored Le Dynasty. The South was ruled by the Nguyen Lords, who became independent and more and more powerful with their territorial expansion southward to the detriment of the dying Kingdom of Champa and the weakened and divided Cambodia.

The Trinh Lords called themselves Princes and Regents; the Nguyen Lords called themselves Dukes and Governors of Thuan Hoa, as they were less arrogant. But the people understood the situation well: The Trinh Lords and the Nguyen Lords were the sovereign rulers, no matter what nobility title they gave to themselves. The people, North and South, suffered tremendously when the two ruling Lords waged wars against one another: Seven times the armies of the Lords clashed causing innumerable casualties and immeasurable destruction.

This story starts right at the beginning of the seventh and last war between the Lords.

[For those who want to know how close the story is to history, an attentive reading of Dai Nam Thuc Luc Tien Bien *may be extremely helpful.]*

*

It all began on the 6th month in the first year the reign of King Le Duong-Duc in Vietnam or the 11th year of the reign of Emperor Kangxi in China (1672). At that time, King Le in North Vietnam was a pathetic toy in the hands of Lord Trinh Tac.

Heaven had announced catastrophes with two omens: first, in the spring, a strange spectacle appeared in the sky with two suns dancing then rubbing against each other as if in mortal confrontation, then one of them disappeared; in the summer, people everywhere could witness the total eclipse of the sun. The men in the street were scared and wondered what the two omens meant. They did not have to wait long for an answer.

The invasion armies marched once more from the North to the border province of Bo Chinh (Quang Binh). The Northern Navy was under the direct command of Trinh Can, the crown prince of Lord Trinh, while the Northern infantry and cavalry were led by the illustrious general Nguyen Thoi Hien.

Lord Trinh Tac, accompanied by King Le, brought up the rear. The Northern armies and navy was ten thousand strong. For propaganda purposes the Northerners claimed that more than eighteen thousand troops were involved.

The smaller Southern armies, initially led by Lord Nguyen Phuc Tan, popularly called the Gentle Lord (Chua Hien), were ready to do battle and repulse once more the aggression from the North. Soon enough, Lord Nguyen surrendered the supreme command to his fourth son, the Marquess of Hiep Duc. Indeed, the battle-worn Lord Nguyen asked his generals to nominate someone to be Commander-in-Chief of all the Southern armed forces and the Marquess of Hiep Duc was chosen by acclamation. Such confidence in his fourth son pleased the Lord as he could never hide his affection for the austere and selfless young man.

*

The Marquess on his knees received the sealed edict from the hands of his father's messenger. He opened it and frowned as he read it. Apparently all the generals of his father had proposed him to be their Commander-in-Chief. But, how could he be the Commander-in-Chief of all the Southern armies at the age of twenty? Hadn't his father favored him too much already by promoting him to *chuong co* (regiment commander) two years earlier, when he was only eighteen? Now, it was the turn of the generals who wanted him elevated, including such an illustrious pillar of the throne, as Nguyen Huu Dat, the Marquess of Chieu Vo, who had for more than thirty years been battling Northern troops and was worshipped by his own troops as well as the population of Bo Chanh Province, who called him *The Bodhisattva*. Bodhisattva means someone who is enlightened and who wishes to attain Buddhahood for the benefit of all the beings endowed with consciousness.

The Marquess thought: "The Marquess of Chieu Vo has learned enough to teach me *the art of war* for the next thirty years; why does he want me to command him? Does he feel revulsion to shed blood now and want to trade in his sword for the monk's saffron robe? Does he want to achieve Bodhisattvahood in this life? Anyway people including his troops have been calling him *"The Bodhisattva."*

He thanked his father's messenger, received respectfully the Commander–in–Chief Dragon Sword from him and sent him away with a verbal answer. He assured his father of his filial devotion and obedience. He expressed his hope that he would not disappoint Lord Nguyen as the commander-in-chief of the armies.

He obeyed his father without hesitation; even though he remembered well a prophecy predicting that he would die young. Would fate raise him to the lofty status of commander-in-chief only to have him killed at the head of his armies?

He said to himself: "I should not think about my fate even for a minute. The fate of my father's Princedom is in the balance. I have to stay focused on that from now on."

He walked out of the main building of his regiment headquarters. His operations hall, with the maps and sand tables and staff offices were all located in that main building. But he had always used a large tent, nearby, as his living quarters. He liked to sleep in the tent with one side open so that he could see the stars at night. It's the 6th lunar month, and the summer weather near the old capital of Ai Tu was often unpredictable. At times, the southern winds blew not only heat but also fine sand into his tent; and at other times muddy water of violent thunderstorms flooded the groundsheet of his tent and his straw bed; but he didn't mind. When the hot southern winds blew, he slept on the groundsheet, enjoying the freshness that came from the beaten earth floor. When his tent was flooded, he simply went to sleep on his large work table. He never complained.

He took his white stallion out of the stable that was built upwind north of his tent and rode off. He always took a long ride when he had a load on his mind. That afternoon, he thought he might need a very long ride. Once outside the encampments of his regiment, he already regretted that he did not bring along the Grand Master's *Ho Truong Khu Co* (Mastery of Strategies by Military Leaders) with him.

For years, he had studied that manual day and night but could not say whether he had understood correctly all the lessons given by the Grand Master. He preferred *Ho Truong Khu Co* far more than Sunzi's *Art of War* or Tran Hung Dao's *Binh Thu Yeu Luoc* (Summary of the Art of War), because the Manual of the Vietnamese Grand Strategist, Marquess of Loc Khe (his real name, Dao Duy Tu, was never pronounced by his direct or indirect disciples) was far more detailed, starting with the simplest advices on weaponry, the casting of cannon, the construction of floating bridges then continuing with bold and original analyses of Heaven, Earth and Man in military terms, explaining advantages and disadvantages of every situation, and finally showing a series of model battle plans.

Since childhood, he had recognized that in order to achieve generalship, he had to master that marvelous treatise.

*

Along his way, some people waved their hands at him. His riding silhouette against the sky was a familiar sight to the local people. They loved him as he frequently went into their small villages to chat with young and old or to bring sweets and toys to the children. A month earlier, the villages were struck by an epidemic of smallpox: he and his troops had, at the risk of being infected themselves, used a crude form of variolation to help save the life of the villagers. The practice that started in China since the sixth century included the use of ground dried scab of smallpox victims and its application to the nose of healthy people.

*

He rode toward the sea. The southern wind parched his mouth, throat and lungs. He rode on along the Thach Han River until he reached the sandy beach near its estuary; not knowing that he had rendezvous that day with his destiny.

In the dry season, in spite of the hot Southern winds that blew inland, high waves came from the Northwest and the North, creating a potentially favorable landing for Northern troops there. The Marquess of Hiep Duc, brought up under the vigilant eyes of his father, had understood when still very young the importance of defending that estuary and the nearby seaport as well as the entire coastline on the Eastern Sea.

While confrontations with the Trinh armies always meant the opposing infantry formations were to stand at the northern border on a   battle line stretching from the sea to the highlands in Laos, it would be a disaster if the Northern Navy succeeded in attacking and razing the Southern fortresses guarding the coastline then moving northward, destroying the Southern rearguards and catching the bulk of the Southern armies in a pincer movement.

The Marquess thought: "Let's leave aside the possibility of an invasion by sea here, let's simply imagine the trouble we will be in if they succeed in landing here a team of spies."

The beach looked deserted that afternoon. Southern fortresses stood every five miles on barren and rocky promontories; the closest one was only a mile away where the Marquess dismounted. Holding the reins of the stallion, he walked down to the water edge. The stallion loved to walk in the warm summer water. The Marquess had not decided yet whether he would walk south or north. Then he noticed two people collecting clams and mussels near the right bank of the estuary, where the sandy beach was strewn with pebbles and rocks.

They were apparently father and daughter, an old man and a young daughter. He did not have the time to ask them who they were before four cavalrymen arrived. They dismounted and went on their knees. The officer among them said: "Forgive us, Your Highness! We did not recognize you from our fortress. We have received your orders to check on anybody appearing on the beach." He sounded a little breathless. He went on after a short pause: "We all are so proud of your elevation to Commander-in-Chief, Your Highness!"

The Marquess smiled and said to himself: "So before the official edict of my father reached me, everybody in the Princedom was already aware of the big event."

The old man and his daughter hearing the officer call the young man "Your Highness" also knelt down and the old man and his daughter chimed in: "Your Highness!" They seemed to tremble a little when they heard the officer mention the Marquess' elevation to Commander-in-Chief.

The Marquess asked the old man pointedly: "Where did you come from?"

But inside him, his mind was in total confusion, because of the voice of the young woman: "That voice! That voice! How could such a voice come from a simple fish woman?" he wondered.

The old man said: "We live a mile from here. We came here by boat. Our fishing boat is moored a little upstream. We caught enough fish today but wanted to pick up some mussels and clams here. At the late evening market, like the early morning market near Ai Tu, customers prefer to buy everything from a single fisherman; so we have to sell a variety of products."

At that moment, his daughter looked up, and for the first time the Marquess saw her face. Her beauty took his breath away. Somehow he felt an immense joy and a sharp pain. He closed his eyes and said to himself: "Be quiet my heart. And you, my eyes! Haven't you seen hundreds of beautiful damsels before?"

Being the most eligible bachelor in the Princedom, he could have any noble girl in the capital city of Kim Long. But he had never fallen deeply in love with any woman before. The eyes the young woman in a split second had shown him depths upon depths of his own soul and colored them with desire and fear, peace and torment. He blurted out: "Your accent, fisherman, shows that you come from Thanh Hoa Province in the North."

The old fisherman bent his head to the ground and said: "Your Highness is right. My grandfather came from Tong Son in Thanh Hoa in the first year of the Chinh Tri reign."

The Marquess frowned: "Those who went south with our Founding Lord, especially those from Tong Son District had found favor in the Southern Princedom and had served in the administration. Why are you a simple fisherman?

The fisherman sensing suspicion in the voice of the young Marquess said quickly: "Your Highness is right again, I too was favored and I served in the administration until my poor wife passed away. I decided then to leave the world and spend my time fishing here and there. My daughter has been kind enough to accompany this poor wanderer."

The fisherman's mere mention of the kindness of his young daughter set fire in the mind of the young Marquess. He stepped back and avoiding setting eyes on her again he asked the officer: "Have you checked their identity?" The officer nodded respectfully: "Yes, Your Highness, they are well known in their village, though they were only passing by. And their boat was searched thoroughly." The Marquess nodded politely to the soldiers, the fisherman and his daughter, and walked away.

He walked his horse along the rim of the water southward now. He knew that he wanted to flee from the scene as quickly as possible. Yet, at the same time, he wanted to know more about the young woman. He wanted to know her name. He wanted to have another look at her face. Then he shrugged and said to himself: "You are going to war in a couple of day. You may die in battle. Forget about *her*."

But he couldn't forget *her*. In a second her upturned face had found its way far into his mind. He knew that nothing, neither time nor space, would be able to erase her loveliness from his memory.

Instead of a quiet afternoon he had thought he needed to plan out his first moves as Commander-in-Chief he was walking now with his head bent down and his heart heavy.

No matter, he had to draw a vast plan to mobilize the rear, and to enhance the strength of the front. In the edict of his father, he saw that an array of brilliant generals and strategists were assigned to assist him. But the Marquess saw that his father did not assign to Nguyen Huu Dat any specific role in the setup. Furthermore, his father did not seem to pay much attention to the rear. Obviously, his father did not want to make all the decisions or to overshadow him and, on the contrary, left him with a multitude of choices to make.

As he walked on with the lead rope in his hand and with the stallion walking contentedly behind him; the high waves from the Northwest made him shudder. He thought about her life on a fishing boat. "How could such a fragile beauty like *her* survive the hardships of a boatwoman's life?" he wondered.

And yet, though he had looked at her just one second he had known that she was not merely a boatwoman. There was so much grace and charm in her look and her voice that could only come from a long line of noble ancestry.

According to the old fisherman's words his forefathers came from Tong Son, the birthplace of the Nguyen Lords clan. Most of those who came from Tong Son with the Founding Lord of the Nguyen dynasty were immediately integrated into the military or civilian services of the Nguyen Lords. That was why he had wondered why the old man and his daughter were mere fishermen, and that was why he asked the officer whether he and his soldiers had checked the identity of both. Apparently everything was in order.

Now, he should focus on the real problems at hand.

The first issue was how to improve the supplies in rice and other foodstuff to the front: He must enlarge three storing facilities close to the front line. The transportation of the supplies was to be done by two fifty-men companies using 37 ox-carts or rather buffalo-carts, each cart pulled by a pair of water-buffalos. In addition, five companies with 150 elephants (easily turned into battle elephants) were to reinforce the transport detachment strength.

He was to launch his armed forces in the 7th lunar month, deploying seven brigades to the defense of the impregnable walls of Sa Phu, Chinh Luy, Tran Ninh, Dong Hoi, Dau Mau, Moi Nai, and the Nhat Le estuary. The strategic plan of the Grand Master was to use those impregnable walls as shields against any invasion from the North. He was sure that if those seven strategic points held fast long enough, then his subsequent lightning attacks on the weakened and discouraged Northern troops would teach the Lords Trinh lessons that they would never forget. They might even end the wars between North and South. Wouldn't *that* be wonderful?

*

He looked back to where he found *her*. Everybody was gone. The desert beach had changed colors. Large flights of seagulls circled and screamed over the water. Their screams resonated in his heart. He had never before felt so much emptiness within himself.

The Marquess mounted his stallion and rode home. An eerie silence surrounded him. He knew that fifty miles to the north, there was no silence. Two armies were going to clash. In the opposing camps orders were being barked, cavalry patrols were circling around the enormous squares of tents; banner bearers were moving from areas to areas transmitting the latest instructions.

His father, Lord Nguyen, at that time of the day, was certainly under the command tent discussing with his lieutenants the newest information gathered by his spies. The Marquess mused: "My father would not move from the advance headquarters until I have launched the southernmost brigades into the war zone and sent through messengers the first orders of the day to all the seven brigades. Then, he would withdraw from the front line, move south, leaving the battlefield and the campaign to me."

"Then, blood would start being spilled. Then, arrows would fly high, whistling through the air announcing hundreds of deaths. Then the cavalry would charge even as the cannon go on roaring. Spears would impale and swords would hack and decapitate. Then, the troops and their officers would mow down the enemy, drunkenly, pitilessly. Then, humanity would recede and bestiality would triumph."

The Marquess went on musing, sensing for the first time in his life that he wanted with all his heart to put a distance between the bloodshed and himself.

In the glow of the sunset, *she* appeared all dressed in white; she smiled to him and beckoned to him. Then she seemed to see what he saw in his mind a minute before and her eyes were filled with tears. He wanted to stop her crying but he knew he couldn't. He said to her: "I am a soldier. My way is the way of the sword. I am good for nothing without my sword, *my love.*"

*

In his tent, under a bright hurricane lantern, the Marquess opened the Grand Master's "Mastery of Strategies of Military Leaders". It was a hand- written copy of the Grand Master's treatise.

He reread the chapter on the use of fire: how to build a fire kite, how to cast cannon shells, how to make smoke bombs, how to launch missiles, how to place land mines, how to use poisonous projectiles, how to make hurricane torches, how to fly flares.

The details described were so clear that even a half-wit could follow the instructions without any difficulty.

The Marquess of Chieu Vo and the Marquess of Thuan Nghia, the two Tigers of the South, who had studied directly under the Grand Master, had used all the lessons learned and reduced Northern troops to ashes times after times.

Somehow on that night the mind of the Marquess wandered and he asked himself: "Should I delight in seeing Northern troops transformed into human torches?" *She* appeared to him with her hands joined. "No, my Prince, the fire with which you burn the enemy could someday turn around and burn you -- and me too."

The Marquess said with tears in his eyes: "May the fire turn around and burn me if it must--but not you, *my love*."

*

A year ago, I saw you for the first time, my Prince. We lived in Ai Tu, the old capital. My life was quiet. I had no ambition, no dream. My father, still grieving after my mother's death—she passed away ten years ago--, led an even quieter life. He read ancient books, played the flute and spent time teaching me about everything. He visited my mother's grave every day. I accompanied him frequently. Cemeteries are not sad places. The wind in the cypress is usually soothing. Bright white tombs, of all sizes and shapes, shine under the sun and assure you that after death, you will rest in a peaceful place. "Life is an exile; death is the homecoming".

My father still worships my mother. But he caused my mother's death. One day, out of the blue, he told her that he wanted to take a concubine. It was normal, as he was a mandarin and all mandarins had many concubines. But my mother did not say anything. She did not show any bitterness or jealousy. She cut down more and more on food and sleep. Soon enough she was a shadow of herself.

My father resigned from the administration and spent all his time by my mother's bedside. But there was not much he could do to reignite her will to live. It took her only a couple of months to die. It will take my father all his lifetime to cry for her.

I was six when that happened. I did not understand why my mother could be so determined to die. After all, my father never took that young woman home. But what I did not know at the time and came to know only eight years later when I was fourteen was that my mother's love for my father was uncommon. Born into an aristocratic family, and well versed in Confucian virtues, my mother whose parents wanted to give away to a wealthy nobleman took the drastic step of eloping and marrying my father instead. Her behavior was roundly condemned by everybody. Her elopement out of love made of her a pariah in high society. Everybody, including her former best friend, shunned her. She accepted without anger the ostracism that made of her a recluse. She lived for her love, for my father and me and never took a step outside our home.

That was why she was mortally hurt when my father mentioned that he would take a concubine. That was why my mother died and my father still lives under a crushing burden of guilt.

Because he has lived for many years under that burden of guilt, he spoils me in every way, as he sees, at every moment, my mother in me.

He has done anything for me. He approves without comments all my foolish dreams. He approves my foolish love for you, my Prince! Even though he knows that my love for you could one day kill me.

*

A year ago I saw you for the first time. It was the day you came to Ai Tu and took command of the provincial regiment. I was in the huge crowd of well-wishers who came to greet you as you entered the gate of your regimental headquarters. You rode in, as handsome, as stern as a war god.

Of course, you could not see poor me. But the second I saw your face I felt I was about to faint. And I knew I would cross a thousand rivers, climb a thousand mountains to be with you, even if it is only for an hour. I knew I would die if that dream dies. I would die if that hope dies in me.

The crowd chanted your name. The troops chanted your name. I was brought by the waves of their voices high up above the clouds. Tears ran down from my eyes: You are my destiny. You will always be.

I told my father about my feeling for you. He listened to me as if I was telling him something really normal and reasonable. But even I... knew that my love for you defied reason. He simply asked in the end: "So, what do you want me to do?"

I said, with shame and pride: "Please find a way for me to come near him, Father!"

He nodded. He said: "I promise I will do what I can." Then, he walked outside and cried.

*

So, the rumors were correct. People said you would ride from your headquarters to the estuary of the Thach Han River many times a month. I had been at the estuary for three days, waiting for you. Then you did come, my Prince. You walked out of my dream and you were more radiant than in my dream. You heard my voice, you saw my uplifted face. My Prince, I knew my voice and my face found favor in your heart. I knew that you found me unforgettable and that your life and mine would be entangled forever.

Then I heard that you were made Commander-in-Chief. Yet everybody knew that my Prince was only twenty. I should be proud of your elevation. But in my heart I trembled for you.

They say that you are a great warrior, that you can fight an army of a thousand men and come out unscratched. But they also say that this time the Trinh Lord brings with him an army of eighteen thousand men. Will you still launch yourself at them at the head of your troops? I trembled for you, my Prince.

*

The Marquess closed his eyes and imagined the Grand Master spelling his five recommendations to his great-grandfather on how to strengthen the South: First, taking advantage of the Hoanh Mountains and the Linh River (together with a system of defensive walls) to protect the South from being invaded; in the meantime, proclaiming the need to restore the power of King Le, and to destroy the House of the usurping Trinh Lords; second, conquering the remnants of Champa's territories, making of the South a bigger country than the North; third, recruiting famers from the North to go south and giving land to them and helping them develop waste lands in the South; fourth, improving the administration of the South and enhancing the prosperity of the entire Princedom; and fifth, recruiting and training soldiers and officers and molding them into a strong army.

The ultimate wish of the Grand Master was the reunification of North and South under the banners of the Nguyen Lords.

The overall strategy of the Grand Master against the invasions from the North was to defend the strategic system of high walls, forcing the Northern generals to sacrifice large numbers of their troops to attack the impregnable walls, then to use light infantry and cavalry to finish off the weakened and demoralized Northern invaders.

He closed his eyes and passed in review the practice of that strategy by the two immediate disciples of the Grand Master's school: The Marquess of Thuan Nghia, the Grand Master's son-in-law, and the Marquess of Chieu Vo, the two pillars of the Nguyen Princedom, both adept in the defense of the Walls and lightning attacks on weakened enemy armies.

The Marquess of Thuan Nghia passed away six years earlier. But The Marquess of Chieu Vo was at the age of 70 still a bold general and a great strategist.

The Marquess of Hiep Duc knew that though he was in command, he must listen carefully to whatever the Old Tiger said. "But the Old Tiger has now been called "the Bodhisattva", how does that jive with his lifelong riding at the head of his troops?" the Marquess of Hiep Duc mused. "How can a warrior be at the same time a monk? How can one wield a sword and psalmody at the same time to the sounds of a wooden fish?"

*

The Marquess of Hiep Duc knew that he had a business that he had to conclude before he could launch his armies and deploy them in the war zone. He had to deal with *her*. He said, addressing to her image in his mind: "Sorry, *my love*, but I have to investigate you and your father, thoroughly. It is possible that you were a team of spies sent by Lord Trinh. It is possible that you were sent as a temptress to conquer me and use me as the principal source of information for the Northern armies. I know, I know, in my heart I cannot conceive the possibility. But as a general, it is my duty to investigate you. I will use one of my lieutenants to be in charge of the case. No information will flow back to me unless they find out that you are really a spy. I will never read your file if you are not a spy sent here to destroy me and our Princedom."

107

He called a confidential messenger into his tent and said: "You will go to the coastal fortress at the Thach Han estuary and give to the commander this verbal order: He has to investigate the fisherman and his daughter that I met this afternoon. All he finds on them, he has to report to my chief of staff, undersecretary of the Department of Governance, Vu Phi Thua. Their file will be marked top secret and kept sealed and locked. No information about them will be directed to me unless it is proven beyond doubt that they are spies. Do you understand my order?" The messenger said: "I understand, Your Highness." The Marquess asked: "Repeat word for word the order."

The messenger was gone. The Marquess sighed and said to the lady in his mind: "I burn to learn everything concerning you. But I cannot use the military services for personal purposes. You will remain a mystery to me, *my love*. No information about you will come to me, because I don't believe that you are a spy."

The thought that he would never find anything about her, *not even her name*, gave him pain. It also gave him a kind of savage joy that he had never felt before. She would always be in his heart wrapped in mystery; the only thing he had from her was the mental image of her uplifted face; but how precious, how gratifying it was!

*

I have convinced my father to take me back to Bố Chánh where the battles would be joined. My father objected strenuously saying that it would be foolish to be there as the two armies advanced toward each other, and the whole Province of Bố Chánh was declared by the Nguyen Lord to be a war zone.

My father's objections were for naught. I knew that he would relent and he did. We sold the boat and took a leisurely ride on a buffalo cart with our meager belongings. We arrived at the beginning of the seventh Lunar month in the District of Tan Thang. We rented a house and waited.

A couple of days later we heard that the Marquess of Hiep Duc, that you, my Prince, had arrived in Tan Thang too.

*

The advance general headquarters in Tan Thang, Bo Chanh Province, pleased the Marquess of Hiep Duc. But he rarely stayed there.

Flanked by the two vanguard commanders, his two chiefs of staff, and the Marquess of Chieu Vo, he inspected all the rows of tents around the headquarters, then rode with them for several days to inspect in their company the seven strategic points on the front line including six defensive walls and a navy engineering battalion that was driving huge piles deep into the Nhat Le River bed, at its estuary, to block the entrance and prevent the Northern Navy fleet from going up the river. The Northern Navy was important in two ways. It could launch a massive attack on the flank of the Southern army; and it was bringing to the Northern army supplies in armament as well as in foodstuff.

The Northern troops were slow in launching the offensive, as Trinh Can, their commander-in-chief crossed the Gianh River only in the 8th Lunar month. But as soon as that took place, the Marquess of Hiep Duc and his generals knew that the waiting time was over.

Then the first battle was fought. It was actually a simple skirmish. But the Marquess of Hiep Duc followed it closely. Trinh Can apparently was a smart strategist. Instead of narrowly focusing on Southern troops commanded by Trieu Tin, Governor of Bo Chinh (Quang Binh) who had withdrawn not only his troops but also the civilian population behind the Dong Hoi Wall; Trinh Can deployed his war machine into a large semi-circle of over five thousand infantrymen and a thousand navy vessels facing not only the Dong Hoi but also the Tran Ninh and Son Dau Walls.

The populations of Bo Chanh were frightened. Lord Nguyen and the Marquess of Hiep Duc launched a propaganda campaign boasting that the Southern troops brought to the front were already over twenty thousand strong and that more were coming. Reinforcements were sent to all the estuaries of the South to assuage the fear of the populations who had never seen so many vessels of the Northern Navy.

Then Trieu Tin made a serious tactical mistake. One afternoon, standing on the Dong Hoi Wall he spotted several Northern reconnaissance units slipping into the Mat Cat Mountain. He turned to his lieutenants and said: "We should sent out troops over there and ambush those units." In hindsight, what he said made no sense as no ambush could possibly be set around a bald mountain. He then made the second mistake: he chose a battalion commander with more muscle than brain to lead the "ambush" party. The "ambush" party got ambushed and the battalion commander escaped with his life, but a large number of his soldiers were not so lucky. Trieu Tin wanted to sentence the battalion commander to death, but the Marquess of Hiep Duc decided otherwise. He said: "Capital punishment is well deserved in this case. However, I want this episode to be treated as an incident of no importance. Let the man go back to his village."

*

In the 10th Lunar month, the generals of the Marquess of Hiep Duc, sensing that major battles would soon be joined, decided to give him a big happy surprise.

They knew what they wanted to surprise him with. They fanned out and looked for the most beautiful young girl they could find. They would buy the girl, maybe, paying fifty pieces of silver after they dazzled her and her parents with the prospect that she could , if she played her cards right on the first night with the princely young commander-in-chief, be taken back to the capital to become his concubine.

They did not have to look far for the young girl. They were soon contacted by a poor old fisherman who wanted to sell his daughter for a hundred pieces of silver. A hundred pieces of silver were a high price for a young girl; but the Commander-in-Chief deserved a high-priced girl. The generals accepted to pay a hundred pieces of silver but they wanted to see the girl first. When they laid eyes on her, they knew that they had seen the most beautiful girl in the entire Princedom.

They were amazed by her beauty, and even more by the intelligence of her answers to their questions. No doubt about it. Their Commander-in-chief should be more than satisfied with such a maiden.

*

My beloved Prince, I have succeeded in convincing my father to sell me to you. Yes, I will be brought to you like a whore, as your generals had paid a hundred pieces of silver for me. Does it matter? I imagine that as soon as you see me, you will understand immediately that I would take any risk to come near you.

I wished I could come to you under other circumstances. I wished I could come to you as a lady. But neither my father nor I could find any other way for me to be put face to face with you.

I know that this would demean me in your eyes. But I hope that when you see me as a woman you will love me. If you only see me as a whore, I will die of shame. I accept to die in shame. But if you relent and take me as a concubine or as a slave-maid, as a lowly slave into your household, then I will be able to serve you a long time, maybe all my life. Then, I would be the happiest woman in the world. To be with you, to serve you every day of my life is my dream, my reason for being. Call me what you want: concubine, maid, maid servant, slave, no matter, as long as I can be with you, I will be more than happy.

On the other hand, if I do not take this golden opportunity to come near you, there wouldn't be another one; and my life would then be meaningless, yes, it would be worthless.

Yet I trembled as they took me to your tent. I trembled as they kept me standing outside your tent and sent in the oldest general to prepare you for the gift.

*

I am on my knees, with my head bent down. I hear your peremptory voice: "Look up, young maiden." I look up. I see you stagger. I see you tremble like a leaf, my Prince. You cannot believe your eyes. Your lips mutter many times: "No, this can't be true."

You look at the generals and said softly but firmly: "Everybody, out of here!" The dismayed generals beat the retreat. Only two bodyguards remain standing, imperturbable, at the opening of the command tent.

You stare at me for a longest time. I see pain and I see joy in your eyes. I see thousands of contradictory emotions ripple through your whole body. Unsure of the final outcome, I stay on my knees as my heart feels like it is going to explode.

At the end you ask: "Why are you here?"

I tremble but succeed in controlling my voice, I say: "I am bought by your generals as a gift to you. I belong to you now."

You blush and there is anger in your voice: "They bought you for a hundred pieces of silver and deliver you to me like a whore. Are you a whore?"

I cry out: "Yes, your Highness, I am a whore, but only a whore for you."

You shake your head: "You are no whore. Why are you here? Are you a spy from the North?"

I say: "I swear on the grave of my Mother that I am no spy."

You pace your tent feverishly for a while then you come back and stand in front of me. You say: "You are not the kind of women who can turn themselves into whores even for a hundred pieces of silver, or even a thousand pieces of silver. And you swear you are not a spy. So what is your motive?"

I cry out: "I would do anything and I would pay any price to come close to you, your Highness!"

My answer startles you and seems to throw you into total confusion. You stand there looking at me as if I am not real. Then you walk slowly to your armchair and sit down. You say: "If you were half as beautiful as you are, I wouldn't hesitate to take you as one of my concubines. (In fact I have no consort and no concubine). But you are too beautiful. Your beauty is overwhelming. Such a beauty can destroy a prince and do harm to a whole nation."

I look up and plead: "I have no power to destroy, to overwhelm or to harm. I would be the happiest woman on earth if you make of me your lowliest slave."

You say: "If you say so! My father was approached by a singer of extraordinary beauty. She told him that she would be contented to be a slave in his household. But soon enough she was raised in ranks and was granted all kinds of titles. She soon had sway over the fate of my father's entire harem. She started arbitrating disputes among my father's courtiers, and had her say in all the decisions of my father. One night my father read Chinese history books and suddenly realized what was happening in his court. The next morning he had her killed."

I throw myself at your feet and say: "I will not seek power. All I want is to be permitted to serve you."

All of a sudden you stand up and call on to the bodyguards: "Take this lady outside and kill her."

I cry out: "If you don't want me to be near you I welcome death. Yes, please kill me, my love."

The bodyguards dragged me to the entrance of the tent. I turn to look at you once more but don't say anything. You stop your bodyguards and say with your raised hand: "Bring her a chair!"

I sit down; my body shakes. You say to the guards: "Go and bring back a hundred pieces of gold, a thousand pieces of silver and ten rolls of silk."

We are finally left alone in the tent. You say: "You came in as a whore bought with a hundred pieces of silver. You will leave my tent covered with gold and silver and silk. They will testify that you are no whore. But I cannot take you as my concubine or maid servant. Soon we will do battle with the Northern armies. There has been a prophecy about me since I was a child: the prophecy said I would die in my early twenties. I am ready to die in battle. Please, don't insist."

Your voice is so calm, so sad. Your words act first like a balm to me. Then they sear my heart. I look into the future and see only darkness.

I cry out: "If you die, I will surely die. Please let me die with you. Please let me die beside you."

*

You covered me with gold and silver and silk. You showed that I was no whore. But you were adamant: I must leave your tent.

I screamed: "Don't send me away. Please, let me be your lowliest slave, or kill me. I cannot live away from you, my Prince."

The flaps of the entrance of you tent were closed. Outside it was dark. You sent me away, not because you didn't love me. You sent me away because you believed that you might die in the near future, that you might die in battle. I wanted to run back to my home put my head in a pillow and scream:" You love me, my Prince. Sooner or later you will send for me. And, I am making another prophecy, my Prince: "You are not going to die."

*

115

In the 11th Lunar month, General Le Thoi Hien of the North attacked the Tran Ninh Walls; the Marquess of Hiep Duc moved his troops to Cu Ha and sent reinforcements to Sa Chuy and the Estuary of the Nhat Le River. The Trinh Lord gave General Le Thoi Hien 3000 more troops and demanded that he captured the Tran Ninh Walls.

Le Thoi Hien dug miles of approach trenches allowing his troops to advance to the Walls.

From the top of the Walls Commander Truong Phuc Cuong saw Northern troops launch thousands of fire balls over the Walls. He also saw how the Northern troops climbing up the ropes and nets to reach the top of the Walls.

He ordered his own troops to use long lances to kill the climbers. He responded the Northern fire balls by using fire kites to create confusion in the Northern camps.

But soon the Northerners forced to win the battle at any costs, mined the foot of the Walls and succeeded in destroying long stretches of the Walls. In one day, the Walls were on the verge of being overrun three times. Commander Truong Phuc Cuong sent messengers to the Marquess of Hiep Duc, asking for authorization to withdraw to the Moi Nai Walls.

The Marquess said: "If we withdraw our troops from Tran Ninh Walls, the Northerners will pursue them and exterminate them before they arrive in Moi Nai. Commander, you have to hold Tran Ninh, I will send reinforcements to you right away."

He dispatched a messenger to Nguyen Huu Dat asking the old general to take the command of the Tran Ninh Walls. For a moment the Old Tiger, designated earlier to the defense of the Sa Phu Walls, doubted the wisdom of his Commander-in-Chief. He saw that Sa Phu had a greater strategic value than

Tran Ninh. He went up to the top of the Sa Phu Walls and looked at the besieged Tran Ninh Walls. From where he was Nguyen Huu Dat could see the desperate situation of Commander Truong Phuc Cuong. It seemed that all the entire Tran Ninh Walls were on fire. Northern cannon kept thundering, Northern infantry men were launching themselves into the battle by the thousands.

Dat thought: "If I do not go there, I know what will happen! The Marquess will personally go there himself."

He called for his horse to be brought to him, and together with the elite elements of his regiment he rode to Tran Ninh.

At a certain elevation he turned around and looked. There! He saw a large body of troops behind him. He recognized the pennants of the Commander-in-Chief.

With his sword he carved quickly on the trunk of a large tree: "I am on my way to Tran Ninh, please go back and hold Sa Phu Walls that I had left almost defenseless." To make sure that the Marquess of Hiep Duc saw the message, he left two flaming torches at the foot of the tree.

He rode on thinking with pride that he had guessed correctly: his Commander-in-Chief would go into the thick of the Tran Ninh battle if he had not done that himself.

He knew that he was riding into an inferno, but he had no regret, and no worry. He had lived his life by the sword; he would be honored to die on the battlefield.

Upon arriving at Tran Ninh he looked back once more. He found that his Commander-in-Chief had gone back to reinforce Sa Phu Walls. Was he watching the fight at Tran Ninh from the top of Sa Phu Walls?

He sped up his battle horse and appeared with his reinforcements at the moment when for the fourth time Tran Ninh Walls were about to be captured. At one place there was a breach of 30 *truong* or 107 meters in the Walls. Dat and his elite troops used their own bodies to plug the breach. They fought like tigers and drove the Northern troops away from the breach.

It was one of the bloodiest battles the old general had ever fought.

The Northern troops pressed on by the promise of gold and the fear of severe punishment fought on desperately as rows after rows of soldiers were mowed down by the elite troops of the Old Tiger.

Night descended on the battlefield and covered part of the gory details from sight. But General Dat had to see where to post his troops and how to plug the breach of the Walls with wood beams and stones and basketfuls of dirt. He ordered hundreds of torches to be lit. In the torch light, the spectacle of the carnage sent shivers to the heart of the veteran warriors, while it scared the novice soldiers to death.

Northern troops fell back and waited for dawn. When dawn came, the gaping breaches on the Walls had disappeared. Heaps of bodies of Northern troops lay by the thousands in the mud from the foot of the Walls to the moats, then the approach trenches, then the clearings beyond those.

Northern troops stood staring uncomprehendingly at the heaps of bodies then raising their eyes to look at their officers. The latter, covered with blood and mud stared back at them, and said: "Let's rest a while then at noontime we will assault the Walls again!" But their troops wondered how they could assault the Walls now that they had seemed to heal miraculously. They had had a chance to capture the Walls the day before, but with the arrival of the Old Tiger General and his elite troops, the chance was gone.

Assaults after assaults ended with defeat. Northern troops, tired and discouraged, ran again and again into the impregnable Walls defended with cannon of all sizes and with squares of well-disciplined and motivated Southern troops.

Bodies of Northern troops kept piling up and became obstacles that slowed down Northern assaults.

Reinforcements came in, but the added troops, most of them new recruits, did not do much to strengthen the Northern forces. The only remaining hope of Northern General Le Thoi Hien was the Northern Navy. If the Northern Navy could break through the defenses of the Tran Ninh estuary, then The Old Tiger General Dat would be entirely encircled.

It was a short lived hope. The Marquess of Hiep Duc ambushed the Northern Navy and destroyed a large number of its vessels.

The Northern Navy Commander-in-Chief, Prince Trinh Can fell ill and his father, Lord Trinh ran northward with Southern troops in hot pursuit.

The Northern infantry around Tran Ninh was encircled by the Southern Navy and infantry reinforced by 60 battle elephants. The bulk of the Northern troops were crushed pitilessly, while small bands of deserters desperately tried to find an escape route. The Southern main brigades under the direct command of the Marquess of Hiep Duc moved in and the carnage was such that carrion birds flew in and darkened the sky and the ground.

Then the rains came down and every path, every village road became a muddy stream. Then rice fields became muddy lakes. The retreating Northern soldiers, the deserters wading in knee-deep mud fell exhausted and were massacred pitilessly by Southern troops.

The carnage was horrible. Remnants of the once-proud Northern troops crossed with tremendous difficulty the Gianh River back to Northern territory. They did not know that it was the last attempt of the Trinh Lords to invade and conquer the South.

*

I have seen too much bloodshed, my love. I sheath my sword and pray that I will never have to unsheathe it ever again.

My brigade commanders performed the body counts ceremoniously and report one after another how many enemy soldiers have been killed, how many have been captured. I read their reports and write laudatory notes to them, while my heart becomes heavier and heavier.

So, this is how a great victory is won, how a war ends! Why does so much bitterness invade my soul? Why do I walk with my head bent down as I visit battalion after battalion of chanting soldiers?

Only a few more days and we will parade in front of my father in Kim Long, the capital city. We will march under unfurled banners and oriflammes. We will hold high a multitude of pennants while the drumbeats will be heard miles away.

Yet I know that most of my men will not enjoy glory and medals, and honors and rewards without the dread of seeing at night the thousands of enemy soldiers piled up sky high and smelling the stench of rotting corpses. Most of my men in the parade will still mourn their comrade-in-arms that they had buried.

I am going home, Father, but I am not going home whole and healthy. I have not sustained any serious injury in the last atrocious battles. But I am coming home filled with shame and regret. I am coming home no longer a warrior. I am coming home to return to you the Dragon Sword. I will never carry a sword ever again.

I may have to put on a saffron robe and pray Buddha for forgiveness. I may have to strike a wooden fish with a mallet at night in my private pagoda and pray for the peace of the wandering souls, ghosts of soldiers we have killed.

*

My father sat down and I sat down. He said: "I know that the country owes you a heavy debt; and I know that you have demonstrated your martial skills, your generalship and your courage to all the soldiers and officers of my armies. I should be asking you about the reasons for all your moves: why did you attack where the enemy was stronger; why did you pull back when the enemy appeared to be weak. You can teach me hundreds of lessons though I have fought a hundred battles myself. But right now I want to ask you a more intimate question: "At the beginning of major battles, one night your generals brought a beautiful young girl to your tent. They had bought her with a few pieces of silver from her father who was broke. I heard that your first move was to ask your bodyguards to take her out and cut her head off in front of your tent. Why did you do that?"

Horrified at myself like every time I remembered the scene, I said: "Actually I stopped the guards as soon as they started hauling her out of my tent."

My father shook his head: "I know that, but why your first move was to have her killed?"

"It hurts more and more whenever I remember the scene, Father", I said. "I had never seen a beauty nearly as perfect as hers. May Guanyin Bodhisattva forgive me; but *she* had Guanyin's beauty. I had never seen a beauty that overcame in a second all the defenses that I had laboriously erected around me to protect the lucidity of my judgment and the integrity of my will. My heart was ready to jump out of my chest, and my knees were ready to bend before her beauty. I immediately recognized in her a goddess and a temptress; someone who had the power not only to destroy me personally but also to potentially ruin an entire nation. That's why I ordered her to be executed, right away."

My father asked: "Did you do that because I myself killed a beautiful woman who enchanted not only me but my entire Court?"

I nodded: "I did hear that story. But the event took place a full year before I was born and no one told me when I grew up what part of that story was fact, and what part, mere legend. I guess you loved her very much and suffered atrociously when she was killed."

My father burst out laughing. But there were tears in his eyes, and he did not care to wipe them away: "My son, I loved her more than anything else in the world; and, yes, my heart is still bleeding day and night for what I did to her."

He stood up and walked around the room. I stood up and followed him with my eyes. He stopped and turned to me: "In the same year, one year before you were born, I killed another extraordinary beauty. *That one was a real snake. And she was so close to sit on the throne* together with her husband, your great-uncle, Nguyen Phuc Ky, Duke Protector of the

Throne, Governor of Quang Nam. She was not his principal consort, but she was so beautiful that in his eyes only she existed. She could have her husband send the principal consort to the darkest jail any time. Sooner or later your great-uncle would succeed to your great-grandfather and ascend to the throne as the Lord, she thought; and she would sit next to him on the throne. Mark you, he was one of the best rulers in history and the Quang Nam population adored him. He could be a great Prince, a great Lord. But Heaven did not allow that to happen. The Duke died unexpectedly. He left behind a beautiful widow that was ambitious, smart and skillful. Your grandfather became Lord instead. The widow of his elder brother used all her artifices, all her cunning to gain access to him. At first your grandfather rejected her advances with indignation. But she kept throwing herself on his path and sending him gifts, until he succumbed to her charm."

My father stopped and, fixing me with his eyes, he asked: "What do you think of that."

I said: "I believe that was clearly a case of incest. My grandfather should have remembered that she was a widow of his brother. By taking her to bed he set a bad example for the people and called upon the nation maledictions from Heaven."

My father nodded: "Even the courtiers, who normally would never say no to their Lord, intervened many times. They risked their life to tell your grandfather that Heaven and Earth would not forgive him for living in sin with that woman, giving her total access to the Court and allowing her to use her influence and her charm to enrich herself. Few people knew it, but her father Tong Phuc Thong, disappointed by the death of the Duke, her first husband, fled to the North and started serving the Trinh Lords. He brought with him a painting of the lady. Both Trinh Trang, the Trinh Lord, and Trinh Tac, the Trinh crown prince fell in love with her instantaneously, and they invaded the South so many times with the desire to see her in the flesh.

Your grandfather should have seen through her and her father's plots. The last time your grandfather defeated the Northern armies twenty-four years ago he did not know that *he had also defeated her.* So when he returned to the capital, he had her onboard his vessel. As they approached the capital, he died. Some people believe that she *poisoned* him to avenge her and her father's defeat."

My father went back to his chair and sat down. He said: "I ascended the throne; and that *snake* knew I would not tolerate her presence in the capital. She went back to Quang Nam Province where for years she led a dissolute life with all the gold she had accumulated under your grandfather's rule. Another great-uncle of yours, Nguyen Phuoc Trung became governor of Quang Nam Province. He had been aware of her past, hated her for entertaining an incestuous affair with your grandfather; he also had suspected her of having poisoned him. Her scandalous lifestyle in Quang Nam was the last drop. He wanted to have her killed."

My father's eyes were filled with anger. He said: "But he couldn't resist her beauty when he finally saw her. Once again she conquered another son of your great-grandfather. She had total sway over him. Soon enough, she succeeded in turning him against me, who had become Lord. She wanted him to rebel against me, plotting to kill me and seize power. I discovered the plot in time and suppressed the rebellion without bloodshed. I could not face executing your great-uncle for treason. I simply put the old man in jail. But I had no qualm whatsoever to have her executed, and to seize all her properties and assets. Her fortune was sold and distributed among the poor."

My father paused and then went back to his initial question: "I asked you why did you want at first to kill that poor child sent gift-wrapped into your tent? Now I want to ask you why did you spare her life then cover her with gold, silver and silk before you sent her away."

I said: "It was not her fault that she was a beauty. She accepted to come into my tent because she wanted to help her father. I gave her the means to help her father without having to sacrifice her honor."

My father said harshly: "Her father had accepted money from your generals. She was sold as a whore. What honor was left to sacrifice?"

Did my father know that he hurt me when he said that? I said: "Yes, I know that her father sold her. My generals bought her like they bought a whore with silver coins and sent her to my tent as a gift. I covered her with silver, gold and silk to tell her that she was no whore to me."

My father said with a cruel smile: "You keep saying to yourself that she accepted to be sold to you because her father was poor. Yet, you know too well that she came to you, not because of her father, but because of her passionate love for you! Her father had little to do with the whole thing. She wanted you; she wanted you to take her as a whore, or as a slave, because she wanted to be loved by you at least once, at least for one night."

I felt my whole body shake and my heart about to break. I said: "Father, please don't talk about her anymore."

My father asked me: "What's her name?"

I said: *"I don't know her name. I didn't ask."*

He insisted: "Haven't you ever tried to find her name and her whereabouts?"

I said: "No, father."

Outside of my father's mansion, I looked up in the sky. I did not know why such a conversation with him made my heart heavy. I mumbled: "*I don't even know her name. I didn't ask*" Why such an admission made me feel so miserable?

THE WOODEN FISH

So my son is gone, my valiant son, the greatest warrior of my Princedom. I still see him on the battlefield, the Angel of Death! I still see him at the age of twenty, who, with the simple title of Marquess of Hiep Duc, was placed at the head of our armies, commanding seasoned Generals who had served three reigns. I saw them competing with one another to shield him from harm with their own bodies.

I saw him kneeling in front of me to report about our victory against the North's invasion, while I covered him with gold, silver and silk. Yet I knew that neither gold nor glory, nor titles nor women, would ever put an end to his quest. He already seemed to have abandoned us and left us stranded where we were while he floated away like a cloud. Oh, my son, my beloved son; why do you have to leave us? Don't you hear the rumors of war once again? Indeed you and your generals have crushed the armies of the North and pulverized their pathetic military resources. But the southernmost region of our Princedom is embroiled in internecine wars between Cambodian kings. Who will lead our armies to go south and pacify those unruly vassals? Why do you abandon everything and put on your saffron robe? Why do you psalmody your prayers, punctuating them with the sound of your wooden fish? Why are you in your thatch-roofed pagoda day and night? Does the sound of your wooden fish cover the new rumors of war?

My son, I too was made commander-in-chief of your grandfather's armies when I was twenty-eight with a mere title of Marquess of Dzung Le. I attacked and sank the first war ships sent to Cua Eo (Thuan An) by the Europeans, more precisely the Portuguese who had entered into a partnership with the Trinh Lord in the North.

Later, I repulsed Prince Trinh's attack on our northern border. But your grandfather passed away in the same year, Oh, Heaven save us! He practically passed away in the arms of "that woman".

My son, you are right, women should not come near us, especially those with great beauty! I had to kill two women of great beauty and I have been haunted over the years by their enchanting eyes.

You are far wiser than me, and you have never loved nor harmed a beautiful woman. And now you have put on your saffron robe! No temptress would go near you ever.

The day your grandfather died, mandarins of the Court named me Commander-in-Chief of all the Naval and Land Forces concurrently Protector of the Kingdom, Marshal of all internal and external affairs, Duke of Bravery.

You are right, my son, the Court will cover you with flowery titles and give you a mountain of honorific functions. But you know and I have leaned to know, we are the Princes and courtiers are there to kowtow to us, flatter us to the point

*of making us puke, and then turn around and ally themselves
with the head of the first rebellion.*

*I want to come to your residence this afternoon. I am
sending my messengers to you now, hoping that I do not come
at a wrong time. I need to talk to you about the affairs of the
Princedom. Do not refuse to see me by staying in your pagoda.*

*

So this is the end of my public life. I leave it without
regret. I look back as far as I could and only see blood and
strife, plots and betrayal. I will wear a saffron robe and live in
my quiet residence.

Behind it I had built a small thatch-roofed pagoda
where in saffron robe I pray for mercy, for forgiveness of the
blood my family had shed, for tens of thousands soldiers of the
North and the South who had died on the battlefields and
where I meditate on the futility of honors, titles, victories and
the horror of civil wars and wars of extermination.

My father whom the people call The Gentle Lord or the
Gentle Prince was stunned when I came to see him and
unveiled my plan to retire from the army and from the Court.
But he had learnt to let me have my way. Once he gave a
counter-order in the midst of my military operations, but I
ignored it and proved myself to be right. Since then he has
never objected to my decisions.

Should I laugh or cry here? I am still full of myself.
Yet, I want to reach enlightenment in one single lifetime. I
want to reach the state of a Bodhisattva in one single lifetime.
Is that succumbing to the worst kind of temptation? Is the
desire to attain Buddhahood a desire? And as long as you still
desire, you do not escape from the cycle of life, death and
rebirth.

Yet, why do I put on this saffron robe, and recite day and night the *Lotus Sutra,* if it is not because I want enlightenment, if it is not because I want to become a Bodhisattva?

Not yet! Not so fast! Before I get anywhere I have to be able to forget *her.* For Heaven's sake, what's her name? I don't even know her name. She came to me in the midst of war, sent to my tent as a tied and bound gift from my generals and her father.

I called my bodyguards and told them to take her outside and cut her head off. Wasn't it the thing to do? My father once sent the woman he loved out with a secret order to kill her, because he knew that an enchantress would sooner or later cause the fall of a kingdom. And she is dead, that enchantress, though her beauty lives on through folk songs and in the memory of doddering old fools who had seen her by my father's side.

But I stopped my bodyguards. *She* was shaking like a leaf. Her eyes held my eyes though. From her body waves of tender reproaches hit me in full force. I was twenty-one at the time, the general commander-in-chief of all the Princedom's armies, but I felt hopelessly vulnerable when she looked at me. Sure I had been around women and had known women carnally. But none of the women I had known, none of the ladies at the Court was in anywhere comparable to her. Her eyes mesmerized me, her trembling lips mesmerized me.

I couldn't keep her as that would be a sign of weakness that would shame me and could be exploited by my enemies. So I covered with her silver and gold and silk and sent her home.

I didn't look up when my soldiers came and escorted her out of my tent, then, out of my camp. But I heard her voice.

I still hear her voice even now: "You don't want to kill this lowly slave. I've found favor in my Lord. So, please keep me, my Lord, as you lowliest slave; but let me be near you, let me serve you faithfully all the days of my life. Don't send me away. I prefer to be killed by your hand rather than live away from you."

Why did she say that? Was she still afraid that I would change my mind again and order my bodyguards to go out and kill her? Was she in love with me? What a ridiculous thought? She only saw me for a few minutes. How could she fall in love with me?

No I have to be able to forget *her* first if I still want to become a Bodhisattva.

Yet, I have to know her name. *I have to know her name before I can forget her*. Without name she will always be a mystery. How can you forget a mystery, or a woman shrouded in the veil of mystery? I have to find her name.

*

My father came with only five escort cavalrymen. He slapped me on the shoulder and asked: "Are you still practicing taijiquan?" I nodded. I loved practicing taiji early in the morning. Even in the rainy season, and when stormy rains made the river water rise, threatening the population of Kim Long with devastating flood, I loved to practice during the lulls of the rain.

My father hated carrying an umbrella, preferring the large brimmed rain hat that covered not only his long hair but also his broad shoulders. My father said: "There is a lull; let's take advantage of that. Let's walk in your jasmine garden."

White jasmine continued to bloom until two months later; then jasmine trees gave themselves a few months of rest. For the moment, the whole garden was embalmed with the fragrance of the jasmine blossoms. My father said: "I have hundreds of advisors, counselors and courtiers who help me solve every military, diplomatic and civil problem. But what I need the most is a wise man that can look me into the eyes and tell me when I am wrong."

I laughed and said: "I am not a wise man, Father, but you can count on me to tell you unvarnished truths."

He stopped and stood under a large jasmine tree. He said: "Only last year you came back to report your overwhelming victory over our enemies in the North. Only last year, I ordered celebrations throughout the Princedom, gave banquets to all the armies, set up altars to thank Heaven and Earth, promoted the local gods, and exempted several districts from taxation. Now the whole Princedom is in a dark mood. Now you are a Buddhist monk. Beyond our southernmost province, our Cambodian vassal kings attacked one another. Though I have sent Nguyen Duong Lam, the son of Duke Nguyen Van Nghia, governor of Quang Binh to settle the matter, I am afraid that the situation will continue to remain unstable."

He looked at me and asked: "What should I do in long term?"

I shook my head: "Father, we will have hundred years of headache if we want to incorporate all the land of Cambodia into our Princedom. Do you know why I have left the army and the Court to live the life of a Buddhist monk? I couldn't sleep after our victories against the Northerners. I saw too much blood spilled in this unending civil war, pitting brothers against brothers. I saw too much suffering inflicted on the Cham people whose only crime was to be born in a country doomed

131

to disappear. I saw how we encroached upon territories of Laos, our ally to the west. I hope that my prayers could reach Heaven and atone for our nation's behavior."

My father looked up the sky. He said: "Do you know how many people died in the last flood right here in Kim Long, right here in our capital?"

I waited for my father to complete his thought. He went on after a long silence: " Floods, storms, fires and wars are all natural calamities. We cannot avoid them. They come to us most of the time against our will."

I said: " I understand that, Father. But hundred years of civil war are not natural; the annihilation of Champa, an empire at one time larger than our entire country South and North; the dismemberment of Cambodia; the annexation of whole Laotian provinces are not natural."

I knew that my father had thought about those matters quite often. I knew that he knew I was right. But as the Prince he had the responsibility of conserving, defending, protecting what he had inherited from his own father. He also had the responsibility to expand his Princedom, expand his influence over vassal kings so that one day he would hand down to his heirs more than what he had received.

I knew that my father wished he could follow my advice. But I also knew he couldn't.

As he was leaving my father asked again: " So, you don't know *her* name?

I said with a tinge of impatience: "No, I don't know father. I didn't ask."

The thinking of my father was circuitous. He had used the technique of coming back to the first question during his interrogations with great success. He asked: "And you haven't tried to find what her name is? Are you sure you don't want to know her name now?"

I regained my composure, I said: "So far I haven't felt the need to find out."

My father smiled, looked out into the vast garden. He said: "That's wise! I know the names of the two beautiful women I killed, and their names have kept haunting me."

I believed that he would not mind my showing a little curiosity. I said: "Nobody has pronounced their names around here; their names have become taboos; can you tell me the name of the lady who ruined the lives of grandpa and my two grand-uncles?"

He laughed: "At the time I executed her she was over fifty; but she looked exactly like when she was twenty-five. Her name is Tong Thi My Anh (Beautiful Queen of Flowers); a really fitting name. "

"What about the lady that you loved and had to eliminate?" I asked. My father frowned but he answered all the same: "The name is Thua. It means to ride, to take advantage of, to receive, to accept, just a very common name. I eliminated her when she explained to me that her name fit into the expression "to ride the wind and crush the wave". She could not help hinting that with my backing she would destroy all her rivals and rule the country."

My father asked again as he crossed the threshold: "Are you sure you don't want to know *her* name and where she is now?" I pretended I did not hear the question.

133

*

I was dyeing my saffron robes. I stood by the large vat and stirred the boiling dye with a long staff. My shami (novice monk) stood by my side trying to learn from everything I was doing. He was as cunning as a fox but pretended to be dumb. That way he could make me repeat my instructions and my orders. But he gave himself away when he executed my orders without fail. I could trust him with the most difficult or most boring task; he would deliver no matter what.

I dyed our saffron robes myself using tubers, roots, bark, plants, flowers, and jackfruit heartwood. Once, my shami told me: "Master! You wield the pole as if you were wielding a fighting staff". I was stunned by his remark. I thought: "It takes a long time to get rid of old habits. Am I still a soldier disguised as a monk?"

I loved my shami like a son, the only son indeed, as I would never touch a woman again. And I didn't touch *her*.

I told him:" Instead of staying there learning nothing, you should be on your way to find out the name of a woman I met two years ago. I don't know her name, and I don't know where she is now. She came to my tent one night when I was about to crush the Northern troops. I sent her away with silver and gold and silk. I did not touch her. I did not ask her name. I was overwhelmed by her ethereal beauty. Could you go and find her and her whereabouts?"

For the first time he confronted me:" Master, are you sure that a Buddhist monk striving for Bodhisattvahood, would want to send me on such an errand?"

I said: "I don't know shami. I don't know what I should or shouldn't do in this case. Would you go and find her?"

My shami said: "I will do anything you order me to do, Master." And away he went.

*

I am the shami of my Master, a novice monk. Flanked by two cavalrymen I rode on, stopping only for short whiles at the horse changing stations. The two cavalrymen and I rarely talked. We knew that we were sent to the northernmost tip of the Princedom on a top secret mission. Failure to keep this secret would mean dishonor or death.

Yet, in my saffron robe I attract attention and fuel curiosity. But I hate taking off the robe and put on a disguise. The cavalrymen carry near the tip of their lances the flame pennants of the Princely Palace Guards. How can a secret mission be conducted with such a lack of secrecy. My Master would say: "Contradiction is at the heart of everything."

The "lady" must be approached with respect. The only question addressed to her must be: "What's your name?"Buddha is my witness! How could a name be so important? Why does my Master stoop to ask such a question? I may never know the answer."

*

"Tracking her proved at first to be almost impossible. We looked into the poor and miserable village hovels. We found no trace of her or her father. The cavalrymen finally suggested: "We have been stupid to look for her among the poor people. When our Lord sent her off, he covered her with silver and gold and silk. We should have looked for her among the rich people."

They were so right! We found her name, Thu Phuong (Fragrance of autumn). We found that she had moved to the capital. We rode back in a hurry to the capital knowing that it would not be easy to find her in our teeming city. We were so impatient to find her that we overlooked many possibilities and nearly lost her track entirely. To our surprise she had become a Buddhist nun. Her religious name now is bhikkhuni Dieu Huong (Mystical Fragrance). Her thatched-roofed pagoda stands just a few streets away from my Master's residence.

The new findings troubled us. We have heard how the lady was dragged away from the presence of my Master, how she implored to be his lowliest slave, how she said death would be better for her than banishment from his presence. Why has she chosen to be so near my Master? It doesn't take a smart man to guess right. She still loves him.

In my shami heart a tidal wave surges, and the roaring waters chant the victorious hymn of eternal love. I weep when I report to my Master. He remains impassible. His lips move and I read on them the names of Thu Phuong and Dieu Huong. Then in the end he says: "That's good. Everything is back in order."

*

I need to see her. I need to see how time and the rigor of monastic life have ruined her Guanyin beauty. It is reported that she has shaven her head. Would a beauty with a shaven head remain a beauty? Certainly not! I need to see *Fragrance of Autumn*. I need to see *Mystical Fragrance*. The two of them merge into one.

But here she is. She has responded immediately to my summon.

She is more beautiful than on that fateful night under my tent. She goes on her knees and whispers: "My Lord."

I regain control of my breath, my heart beats and my composure. I tell her to get up. I direct her to a chair and ask her to sit down. Until then she hasn't cast a glance at me. Now she looks up. Her Guanyin beauty took away my breath.

My father told me once: "Never trust a woman whose beautiful eyes deprive you of all distinction between good and evil. Never trust a woman whose beauty takes over your free will. If you find such a woman on your way, you must have the courage to kill her."

Perhaps he was right if he talked about men with absolute power, afraid to let go parts of their authority, or afraid to see the ruin of the fragile nation they rule over.

But I am now a private person. The destiny of nations no longer is my concern, and all my true desires are gone. I don't have to fight beauty and its destructive potential. I am a monk in my saffron robe.

I know that the woman in front of me has all-powerful eyes. But I read in her eyes more than her sway over me. I read in them the calm and deep compassion of an enlightened soul. She says: "May the Lord Buddha grant you, Your Highness, all the blessings that you more than deserve." It is a banal formula of courtesy. But I know she means it. I say: "Monastic life suits you, bhikkhuni Dieu Huong. You are more beautiful now than when I met you the first time."

Does she blush? I am not sure.

I ask her: "Do you know that my garden is full of jasmine blossoms right now? The entire garden exhales the lush *fragrance of autumn.*"

137

She says: "May the fragrance embalm your life. May it follow you on the path to enlightenment and Bodhisattvahood?"

I said with an audible sigh: "I found the path to enlightenment a year ago under my tent."

She is obviously troubled by my remark. She looks at me then quickly averts her eyes and says in a whisper: "That evening I told you I would always want to serve you as your lowliest slave. My saffron robe *doesn't change that. Nothing can change that.* But I know now that our lives will *merge* only when we both attain Bodhisattvahood."

I want more; I want to hear more. But her soul that a moment earlier opened up like a blossom with all the petals deployed has closed itself up. I know, I know that silence penetrates deeper than words.

Anyway, is there anything left unsaid?

*

She is gone. The fragrance of autumn still lingers. I go to my thatch-roofed pagoda. I sit down, pick up my wooden mallet and strike my wooden fish rhythmically while I chant *Om Mani Padme Hum* and invoke the name of Amitabha Buddha. My mind follows the curls of scented blue smoke that rises from incense sticks planted in a large ceramic bowl.

From a distance I hear the sounds of another mallet striking a singing bowl, *her singing bowl*. There is a long space between its sounds as if to tell me that spacious nothingness spans over existences. The sounds respond leisurely to my hurried beats on the wooden fish. Is there anything purer than those sounds from her singing bowl in all the Pure Land?

Two solitudes entangle, two disembodied existences merge. Why wait for the attainment of Bodhisattvahood? The here and now is more than satisfying. Nothing to desire, nothing is missing. Why is there the need for Nirvana? I look into the void and see eternal contentment. I see Death waiting at the door. I will invite Death in when it's time.

(The young Marquess of Hiep Duc died a year later in the 6th lunar month at the age of twenty-two, like the prophecy that had predicted his early death since he was a child. Some legends say that bhikkhuni Dieu Huong died two months later, at the age of twenty-one).

In Memoriam

To my friend Nguyễn Văn Vĩnh

There was a time when the phone rang

My soul responded but my hand delayed

the moment you started greeting

As the fear mounted.

I did not know what horizon we would search

What depth we would go to find the beginning of a question.

I did not know how much soul searching would be involved

whether I had the strength that particular day to follow your drift.

So many questions we asked

So few answers we found!

Yet each call you made filled my day with fear and savage joy.

Now you are gone and my line went dead

Who will talk to me about God, and Hell, and Hell on earth?

Who will talk to me about sin and redemption?

I reread the books we read together

turning the yellowed pages.

I walk alone among the live oaks

Thinking about so much exploration

So much pain we shared.

All I can do is to look at the people you loved

Who feel the same way the emptiness around us.

All I can do is to listen to their excited litanies of the joys in time past.

But there will be an end to all this

When the stars shine around us

When the suns and the moons revolve under our feet

Among the fleecy flocks of white clouds.

And then we will renew our discussions

Momentarily interrupted.

Then there will be fewer questions

and many more answers.

There will be more light than darkness;

There will be more shine than rain.

I will stand and contemplate a beautiful soul chiseled by our Maker;

And those who loved you and miss you

Will sing in unison

To the music of angels.

André Nguyễn Văn Châu

About ANDRÉ NGUYỄN VĂN CHÂU

Andre Nguyen Van Chau was born in the Citadel of Hue, the old capital of Imperial Vietnam. He grew up with classmates who have become known writers, poets, composers and painters.

After obtaining a doctorate degree in the humanities at the Sorbonne, Paris, he taught English and creative writing at various universities in Viet Nam for twelve years.

In 1975 he began twenty-five years of work for migrants and refugees around the world, ten of which were spent as the head of the International Catholic Migrations Commissions with 84 national affiliates and with headquarters in Geneva, Switzerland.

He has traveled and worked in over 90 countries.

Back to the United States after Geneva he was for ten years the Director, Language and Accent Training at ACS, then Xerox before retiring in Austin, Texas and beginning a new career as a full-time writer.

One of his published works, *The Miracle of Hope,* has been translated into eight different languages.

The New Vietnamese-English Dictionary, on which he spent an inordinate number of hours over more than twenty years, was finally published in 2014.

In 2015 *A Lifetime in the Eye of the Storm ,* published originally in 2003, was revised and published.

Journeys into Darkness and Light, a collection of short stories and poems was published in April 2015. It is followed closely by *Night and Day,* another collection of short stories.

He and his wife, Sagrario, have four children: Andrew, married to Jodie Scales, Boi-Lan, married to Rodolphe Lemoine, Michael, married to Rachel La Fleur and Xavier. They have seven grand-children: Katelyn, Géraldine, Alix, Drew, Noah, Isabelle and Luke.

Other Books By This Author

Journeys into Darkness and Light

Born in Vietnam in 1935, André Nguyễn Văn Châu grew up in the midst of wars; enduring intense emotions ranging between hopes and disappointment to joys and sorrows. Many of the stories he penned in 'Journeys into Darkness and Light' set tragic characters against terrible odds. Most of them triumphed over their despair, or accepted their demise with superhuman courage.

Later in his life the author lived and worked in scores of countries where men and women from different parts of the world, especially in Africa, shared the same joys and sorrows with their Vietnamese contemporaries. He spoke of them and shared their stories with the same tenderness, complicity, and emotional intensity.

The brevity of these stories considerably enhances the general theme. It highlights the loneliness, alienation, terror in the face of the passing of time and death, in the characters, and also their surging moments of happiness and hope.

A Lifetime in the Eye of the Storm

History is colored by the nation that is recording it. In America, the Vietnam War was chronicled in the newspapers and on television. The heart breaking stories we heard were always about the war from the American viewpoint. When we are able to view historical events from perspectives other than our own, we begin to understand that the important thing isn't winning or losing, but learning and understanding.

Hiep lived her life, from earliest childhood, at the center of the war. This is her story of love and loss, triumph and tragedy. It is the story of all women who have lived through a war, with only their steadfast love, hope and faith in God to give them the strength to go on living.

A Lifetime in the Eye of the Storm is based in fact on the collective memory of the members of the Ngo Dinh family. The author had collected the details of the story in thousands of hours of interviews with them.

Each member of the Ngo Dinh family contributed to the final product with their different perspectives, their personal opinions and their points of view.

This second and revised edition offers hundreds of pictures of the Ngo Dinh family and historical personalities who played a major role in the achievements and the tragedy of the family.

"It is a moving account of the Ngo Dinh family's determination to live and work for the freedom of their beloved country."

The Miracle of Hope

Known to many Catholics through his writings (Testimony of Hope; The Road of Hope), Vietnam's late Cardinal Francis Xavier Nguyen Van Thuan's amazing story is told by a former fellow seminarian who knew him from the time the cardinal was 18. Chau initially declined the cardinal's request to write about his life, but in 1999, reluctantly agreed, finishing the book just a few months before the cardinal died in 2002. Chau has meticulously chronicled Cardinal Thuan's life and that of his prominent family, which paid dearly for its involvement in the quest for Vietnam's independence. To help the reader navigate through a complex cast of characters, Chau has included a glossary and an explanation of Vietnamese personal names. He portrays Cardinal Thuan as a humble man who gladly would have served as a rural pastor, but was marked for leadership in the church early on. Even as he prepared for this role studying in Europe, Cardinal Thuan had a premonition that he would suffer martyrdom, and indeed, after being named coadjutor archbishop of Saigon in 1975, he was arrested by Communist authorities. Thuan subsequently spent 13 years in prison, which shaped his spirituality and leadership. ~ *Publishers Weekly*

The Holy See has started Cardinal F.X. Nguyen Van Thuan's cause for beatification.

In 2013, Pope Francis said: *"In effect, there are many people who can attest that they were edified by their encounter with the Servant of God Francis Xavier Nguyen Van Thuan, at different moments of his life. Experience shows that his reputation for holiness has spread precisely through the testimony of so many people who met him and [who] preserve in their heart [the memory of] his gentle smile and the greatness of his soul. Many came to know him through his writings, simple and profound, which reveal his priestly spirit, closely united to the One who had called him to be a minister of His mercy and His love. So many people have written to tell of graces [received] and signs attributed to the intercession of the Servant of God Cardinal Van Thuan. We thank the Lord for this venerable brother, son of the East, who ended his earthly journey in the service of the Successor of St. Peter."*

The Miracle of Hope has been translated into Italian, French, German, Spanish, Portuguese, Polish, Japanese and Korean.

The New Vietnamese - English Dictionary

This is an advanced Vietnamese dictionary with English definitions, compiled with the enrichment of the Vietnamese language, and its preservation in mind.

This dictionary lists words and expressions used by Vietnamese throughout the ages. It shows local and ethnic dialectal words and phrases and promotes the understanding of the Vietnamese culture past and present.

With over 1170 pages, it is the most comprehensive collection to date.

Its entries cover all the words that have been used by Vietnamese since the fifteenth century. It's a colossal research work in the fields of ichthyology, ornithology and botany. The precision of Vietnamese terms in these fields is enhanced by the use of Latin scientific names.

The dictionary attempts to cover all the new sciences and technologies using Chinese terminology only when it is absolutely necessary.

It also attempts to provide the maximum number of non-Chinese loanwords.

It also provides words of the larger ethnic groups in Vietnam, especially the Muong, which is very close to the Vietnamese culturally and linguistically.

It does not attempt to address etymologic issues as elements are still missing in the context of current linguistic knowledge, especially historical semantics, but wherever possible, the etymology of the words is offered.

The dictionary is a great tool for scholars, translators and interpreters. It is also a great tool for English-speaking students who want to learn Vietnamese seriously.

www.ingramcontent.com/pod-product-compliance
Lightning Source LLC
Chambersburg PA
CBHW051150260626
47170CB00005B/2047

9 781941 345559